PRAISE FOR SWEAR ON THIS LIFE

"*Swear on This Life* is Renée Carlino at her finest. Raw, real, and gripping; I read it in one sitting."

—Colleen Hoover, #1 *New York Times*
bestselling author of *It Ends With Us*

"Carlino fans will love this one, and so will readers who have not yet made her acquaintance. The tale is engaging and paced to keep the pages turning long after the lights should be out."

—*Kirkus Reviews*

"Mysterious and compelling, *Swear on this Life* is the epic love story your summer needs."

—*Bustle.com 11 New Romance Books
Perfect for Summer Beach Reading*

"Romance fans will find this heartfelt story of resilience and first love hard to put down."

—The *Library Journal*

"Readers... will find themselves simply smitten by both the novel in front of them and the story within the story. Romance readers and women's fiction fans should snap up this charming love story."

—*Booklist*

Praise for BEFORE WE WERE STRANGERS

LIVING MAGAZINE "NEW ROMANCE CLASSIC" PICK

LATINA MAGAZINE PICK

"*Before We Were Strangers* is as steamy as it is sweet. With two characters who are meant to be but just can't get the timing right, Renée Carlino has mastered the missed connection. I found myself rooting for Matt and Grace at every turn and aching to crawl into the book to go back to the 90s to join them. Evocative, tender, and satisfying, Carlino has outdone herself."
> —Taylor Jenkins Reid, author of *Maybe in Another Life,*
> *After I Do,* and *Forever Interrupted*

"Powerful and poignant, *Before We Were Strangers* captures the magic and heartache of first love. I couldn't turn the pages fast enough."
> —Tracey Garvis-Graves, *New York Times*
> bestselling author of *On the Island* and *Covet*

"This is one of the most romantic, heartfelt, and consuming books I've ever read. To say that I'm in love with it would feel like the biggest understatement ever... I'm blessed, so insanely lucky, to have found a story that I finished reading with tears in my eyes and a more beautiful outlook on life, love, and believing in second chances."
> —*Book Baristas*

"Exquisitely written... I highly recommend this if you're in the mood for a really great, heartfelt journey loaded with angst and healing, all in the name of true love."
> —*Maryse's Book Blog*

PRAISE FOR AFTER THE RAIN

"Renée Carlino's writing is deeply emotional and full of quiet power. You won't be disappointed."

—Joanna Wylde, *New York Times* bestselling author

"*After the Rain* tore me up in the best way possible. Sexy, sweet, and sad, all woven together with an overwhelming undercurrent of hope, Nate and Avelina's story is one that goes straight to my list of all-time favorites."

—Amy Jackson, *New York Times* bestselling author

PRAISE FOR NOWHERE BUT HERE

"There is a certain 'magic' or 'spark' or whatever you want to call it that really makes a book come to life as you read it. As a reader, I'm on a constant search for that special spark, and I absolutely found it here. *Nowhere but Here* was a unique and beautifully written love story. I laughed, I swooned, I wiped happy tears away, and I fell in love. This book warmed my heart and left me with the most wonderful feeling. I highly recommend it for all fans of romance!"

—*Aestas Book Blog*

"The kind of romance that gives you butterflies in your stomach, that tingly feeling all over, and a huge smile on your face... If you are looking for something emotional, where you can truly experience what the characters are feeling through the beautifully written words of an amazing author, complete with a wonderful epilogue that will give you a sense of completeness, then look no further."

—*Shh Mom's Reading*

PRAISE FOR SWEET THING

"Sassy and sweet, *Sweet Thing* melts in your mouth and goes straight to your heart!"

—Katy Evans, *New York Times* bestselling author of *Real*

"Surprisingly, this is Renée's debut novel because she writes like a pro with words flowing effortlessly and beautifully, totally hooking me from the beginning. There was something intangibly real and special about this book, which kept me reading until I finished it... one of my favorite stories of the year."

—*Vilma's Book Blog*

LUCIAN DIVINE

RENÉE CARLINO

Felicia,
Angels are
everywhere!
xo, Renee
Carlino

For my parents, whose faith is as strong as their sense of humor

LUCIAN
DIVINE

PREFACE

WHEN I WAS about four years old, my sister and I made up this rule that we couldn't lie if we said, "Promise and lying is a sin." I would say, "I didn't take your cupcake off the counter," and she would say, "Promise and lying is a sin?" And I would confirm, "I promise and lying is a sin." It was our version of, "You Swear to God?" Of course we weren't allowed to swear to God—we were Catholic. It was a weird phrase that we made up to mean the same thing, and before long, the phrase blended together to sound like one word—*promisinlyinsasin.*

After a while, we stopped thinking about the meaning of each word. What is a sin? What is a promise? What is a lie? It became a truce between sisters more than a truce with God. At first, it was a reminder not to lie because you'd go to hell for sinning, but it became a reminder not to lie because, plain and simple, when we lie, there are consequences here on Earth with the humans we love.

During my first holy communion when I was six, a little

boy in my Catholic school was chosen to carry the wine to the altar during the special mass. You know, the blood and body of Christ? He tripped and fell in the aisle, subsequently tossing the wine into the air before it went crashing onto the stone floor, splattering the blood of Christ on three little girls wearing their white communion dresses. It was impossible, even at the age of six, for me not to laugh at the irony. The nuns were furious, the boy was mortified, and the three girls were in tears because they didn't look *pretty* anymore... not with Carlo Rossi staining their satin and lace.

When I was growing up, my parents watched and loved a few movies that portrayed holiness or God or heaven in some way. Honestly, it confused me that my mother would say some jokes were sacrilegious, and then she would laugh at movies like *Oh God!* with George Burns and John Denver. *Michael*, with John Travolta, was another one I remember. Also, *Defending Your Life*, with Albert Brooks and Meryl Streep.

I love the romantic quality of the movie *City of Angels*, with Meg Ryan and Nicolas Cage, which my husband constantly reminds me is a remake of the Wim Wenders film, *Wings of Desire*. I always thought it was insanely romantic to be chosen the way Meg Ryan was in that film. No one else could possess what she had. It was something so prevalent and unique that even an angel would give it all up.

I mention movies because I always see my books as movies. That's how I imagine them, so in writing this book, I thought about a lot of movies that gave me inspiration. Like *Beetlejuice*, where the afterlife is portrayed with such unrestrained creativity. I imagined the writers bouncing hilarious ideas off one another, letting their imaginations fly.

I laughed to tears at Silent Bob and Chris Rock being prophets, while Ben Affleck and Matt Damon were fallen angels without a clue in *Dogma*. And not to be forgotten is Alanis Morissette playing God.

It's all profoundly hilarious to me that no matter what you believe in, no one actually knows anything for sure. But if you have an imagination that surpasses what you've been taught about God, then there are endless possibilities for what might exist above us, below us... beyond us. It's fodder and faith and all that is unknown, and it still amazes me that faith alone holds the key to religion everywhere, all over the world. Faith is strong enough to die, to kill, and to sacrifice for. Faith alone.

Whether you're religious, spiritual, agnostic, or atheist, there are some absolute truths about life in this book that have nothing to do with religion at all. I knew that I might offend some people with this content—they might even call it sacrilegious—but I assure you, I wrote every single word with the sense of humor that God gave me. This book is not about God or angels. This book is about faith, love, the unknown, and not taking ourselves so damn seriously all the time.

1

BIBLE
Evelyn

BROOKLYN USED TO talk incessantly about the rules of dating. She had so many that she couldn't remember them all, but the first few were the most important. Rule number one: never seem overly eager. Don't act interested!

"You have some kind of tech job, right?" I asked. "We talked about it last time. Where do you work again? And what is it that you do?"

"I work in Internet security, in San Jose," Beckett said.

My nerves were swirling furiously in my stomach and bubbling up in my throat. I liked this guy. I thought he liked me. I hadn't felt that way in a long time. "Internet security, what is that exactly?"

"I write programs that people download to protect their

PCs from viruses and stuff," he said, smiling, his eyes crinkling at the corners.

Does he feel sorry for me that I don't know what Internet security is?

It was my third date with Beckett, the first guy I had been out with more than once since graduating from fashion school. Actually, the first guy I had been out with more than once... ever. Our two prior meetings had been casual double dates with my roommate, Brooklyn, and randoms Josh and Swayze—yes, like Patrick. His mom had a thing for the movie *Dirty Dancing*.

Double dates with Brooklyn and whoever usually involved a lot of eating, drinking, semi-existential conversation, some pot smoking, hooking up, passing out, and everyone happily going to Bloody Mary brunch the next day... then never talking again.

"It's the only way," she would say. That brought me to her second rule: never go out with the same person twice.

I didn't understand the point of dating if you weren't trying to get to know someone, but Brooklyn seemed happy and I never had any luck with guys, so I had begun taking her (not always helpful) advice. Brooklyn came from a progressive family. Her parents had an open marriage. Monogamy was never really valued in their household, so to Brooklyn, dating was like a game. A game she wanted to win. My best friend since childhood equated marriage to an agreement involving taxes and sometimes children. Her third rule—never entertain marriage unless he has a trust fund— was probably the worst, but it didn't matter because how could you even get to entertaining marriage if you were following rules one and two?

After living with her for few years, her rules started making more and more sense to me. She was happy and free and life seemed uncomplicated for her. Once I started following her rules, we had the time of our lives. But then I met Beckett. Something about him kept me responding to his texts and saying yes to hanging out. He showed promise. When I was with him, I thought about my future more than Brooklyn's rules.

"So this is officially our third date?" Beckett asked as he reached across the table to take my hand.

It *was* our third date... technically. But it was the first without friends tagging along. We were at Blackbirds, which is mostly cocktails in a dark room. Beckett was sipping a fancy Scotch thing, and I had an eight-dollar, four-ounce jalapeno margarita.

"I like how cheap the drinks are here," I said, ignoring his comment and pulling my hand back. Eight dollars *was* in fact cheap for a margarita. In the Bay Area, everything is expensive, especially being young.

Beckett and I hadn't slept together. We had done other things back at my apartment, but nothing serious; he had been a true gentleman. I often caught myself batting my eyelashes at him like a fucking idiot, but I was smitten and that feeling was all new and shiny to me.

He had the head-to-toe look that made Brooklyn go crazy, complete with a forearm tattoo of a random pinup girl sitting next to a bottle of ketchup. She had been into him first, but he hadn't shown interest in her, which for some reason made me like him even more. Brooklyn was hard to look past. She had that confidence thing going for her.

"I like that," I said, pointing at the ketchup bottle tattoo.

"Kind of a Warhol homage," he said.

"Yeah, I figured." I smiled and batted my stupid eyelashes again.

He was into me and not Brooklyn, and I wondered if that was driving my attraction toward him. I wouldn't say I was ever second fiddle, but I let Brooklyn believe that. Being a novelty was a turn-on to her. She was easygoing, intelligent, pretty, and she got a lot of attention, which she needed all the time. Brooklyn would get naked with almost any guy who had a beard and a Mohawk and showed interest in her. If he wore suspenders, he was an automatic shoo-in. Beckett had all of those things, but I was the one he'd set his sights on the night we met him.

We had been hanging out at an old-school dive bar on Market that was usually swarming with hipsters. Brooklyn was the kind of girl who knew showing off her legs in San Francisco was sexier and more exotic than hiding a tiny bit of cellulite. The night we met Beckett, Brooklyn was wearing high-waisted cutoffs rolled up to her ass, boots, and a maroon fedora. I'd had on some variation of black on black because, while I could design high fashion, I never cared to wear it. Brooklyn said I was going all Vera Wang on her, but I just found clothing shallow beyond the art of design.

The truth was that I was insecure for no reason. I didn't like attention the way Brooklyn did. But my black on black and wanting to blend in with whatever wall I was standing against didn't bode well for my love life.

That first night when Beckett approached me at the bar, I thought he'd ask about Brooklyn—I was used to that—but he didn't. He asked about me instead, and now we were on our third date, talking each other's ears off.

"I've been working for this woman, Tracey. She's a headache. She wants to do a denim line, and I want to cut off my ears every time she brings it up. She's been on the circuit with these T-shirts—they're basically like fifty-fifties, and she acts like she invented the damn shit." I rambled on while Beckett looked totally enthralled. "She's always trying to get in on stuff after it's already been done. It's one thing to know what's trendy, but it's real talent to know what's *going* to be trendy... I think."

"Yeah, I get that. It's the same in my job," he said. "You have to be creative with these programs, stay five steps ahead of the shitheads writing viruses. If you don't like Tracey, why don't you do your own thing?"

"I am. I mean, I'm always sketching. I just need the money right now. I have to stick it out with her for a while until I can get my own studio. She got some Japanese denim in last week and came up to me saying we needed to do a high-waisted bell-bottom. I said, 'You mean like the jeans that are in every single store right now?' She's seriously stifling my creativity. She's sucking the life out of me."

"That's a bummer. Don't let it discourage you. I saw some of your designs last weekend, and they're totally deck."

"Deck?"

"Yeah, like fresh."

"Uh-huh. Thanks." I nodded, wondering how I'd missed the memo. *Damn hipsters.* "Do they have food here?"

"I don't think so. You hungry? Want to go to 4505?"

"Yeah, let's do it."

4505 Burgers & BBQ on Divisadero was a casual meat-fest. I had a root beer float, and Beckett and I shared a half a platter of ribs. There was meat and BBQ sauce in his beard through our entire meal, and it didn't bother me one bit. I found it charming. Again, all new and shiny feelings. I had only slept with two guys in my entire life and neither was memorable at all, so at twenty-four, I felt inexperienced. But Beckett was sweet and easy to be around.

Afterward, walking toward my apartment, we popped into a local hole-in-the-wall bar to grab one last drink before I invited him up, though he didn't know yet that I had planned to finally have him over. It was only eleven, and I knew Brooklyn would be out until two in the morning at least.

The bar—which by the way had no name—was a cool little place to get in one last drink. The bartenders dressed up in *Star Wars* costumes... always. It was just their thing. Tonight the bartender was Han Solo. When Brooklyn or I referred to the bar, which only had a neon sign with bright yellow letters reading Cocktails, we called it the Star Wars bar.

Beckett and I sat at a table across from the bar top. I ordered a glass of wine.

He, of course, ordered the *hoppiest* IPA then said, "Hoppy makes me happy."

I laughed as the bartender walked away.

"Bad joke?" he said.

"I'll let it slide."

Only a few loners were sitting at the bar, but the music coming from a jukebox in the corner was really loud.

"They should turn it down, huh?" I yelled.

"You want me to ask?" Beckett yelled back.

"Would you?"

"No problem." He got up and headed toward the bar.

I saw him exchanging words with the bartender, then a man sitting at the end started talking to Beckett as well. I stared down at my drink and wondered if more alcohol was a good idea. When Beckett came back, the music was still hauntingly loud, playing "Bad Love" by Eric Clapton. I felt as if we were in a cheesy motorcycle movie. Beckett was bobbing his head to the beat and smiling. His demeanor had changed.

"What did they say?" I yelled.

"He said it's a fixed volume. They can't change it!"

"What? That's insane! I've been in here other times and the music wasn't this loud!"

"But it's Clapton." He was still bobbing his head.

I appreciated his enthusiasm, but I didn't feel like yelling over Clapton while I was trying to get to know Beckett. "What did the other guy say?"

"The guy at the bar?"

"Yeah!"

We were still yelling across the table, ridiculously.

"He was wasted. He said these were his picks and to fucking leave it, and then he rolled his eyes at me and said something like, 'Elders are gone from the gate, young men from their music.' He touched my forehead. I almost fucking slapped him." Beckett looked at the ceiling. "The music is good though."

He must be kidding. "Is that a biblical reference?"

"This song?" he asked, pointing up to the ceiling again.

"No, what the guy said."

We were missing the mark. Our conversation was becoming more and more awkward by the second. The date was going downhill fast. All the smitten, shiny feelings were beginning to dull. This always happened to me.

He shrugged. "No clue, man."

Did he just call me "man"?

The next song came on, a slower, quieter acoustic ditty sung by a familiar voice. Beckett pointed at the speakers yet again and shouted, "Fuck yeah, Tom Waits!"

It was the song "I Hope That I Don't Fall in Love with You," and Beckett knew every word. He serenaded me with his hand on his chest while I looked around for a hidden camera.

"Am I being Punk'd?" I asked.

"What?"

"It's just that you're pointing at me and saying you hope you don't fall in love with me."

He shook his head as if I were confusing him. "I'm singing. What's the big deal?"

"Never mind!" I yelled. "Do you want to go to my apartment?" The music came to a screeching halt while I was mid-sentence, basically broadcasting my proposition to the entire bar.

Beckett looked affronted. First time I'd offended a guy by inviting him over.

"But the music is so good here," he said.

A moment later, the music was back on, and I swear it was even louder than before. I nodded, although I had never been so dumbfounded in my life. "Okay."

I finished my wine and watched Beckett continue, song after song, to flip out in excitement over the music.

One o'clock and three glasses of wine later, the jukebox was still blaring random selections, even though I hadn't seen anyone go near it. There were four barflies on stools and

Beckett and me at a table, while the rest of the place was empty. My mind was clouded by his strange behavior, and my patience was growing thinner by the second. I had had enough.

"I'm going home!" I yelled.

When I stood, he smiled. He didn't bother standing. He held up his hand and waved.

"See ya!" he shouted over "Sad Angel" by Fleetwood Mac.

What in the hell just happened?

I was eager to get home to make sure I didn't have a giant fleck of lettuce in my teeth. Apparently, Beckett was no longer into me—he was into classic rock. I walked two blocks and up two flights of stairs into my lonely, dark apartment. Brooklyn was still out.

We had a corner in the Mission, which was expensive, but her very progressive parents were still paying for half of it, so we split the other two grand. That meant we had the nicest rental for the smallest amount of money in the area. It was a typical San Francisco third-floor apartment with a round-corner living room. Our place would have been amazing had Brooklyn not been the biggest slob in the world.

I didn't turn on any lights; I just stared out the window onto the street and played back the date in my mind.

Did I act too whiney about the Tracey situation? Was I eating the ribs like a barbarian? Did he get a better look at my body and notice the saddlebags?

I needed to stop obsessing, but I was still confused. Within a couple of hours, I had gone from *I think this guy is going to be my boyfriend* to *I think this guy is clinically insane.* I thought I knew him. I thought he liked me. I was seriously questioning my own character judgment.

Brooklyn's rules were running on a constant loop in my head, but still, I was undeterred. I needed to know what went wrong with Beckett. I had made up my mind; I was going to confront him.

Stringing my purse across my chest, I skipped right back down the stairs and headed to the bar where I had left Beckett singing his heart out. The moment I walked through the door, I noticed the music was no longer blaring, the lighting was a little brighter, and there were at least fifteen more people at tables and at the bar itself. It had become a completely different place in less than thirty minutes. Buckley was crooning softly from the speakers, and Beckett was nowhere to be found.

A moment later, my phone pinged with a text from him:

Beckett: *Sorry about tonight. I don't know what came over me. It was like I was stoned in that bar, pullin' a total Jerry. I'm really am sorry.*

Me: *It's cool.*

But really, it wasn't cool. Pulling a Jerry? Seriously? Speak English. I didn't know why I was back in that stupid bar looking for him anyway. I was currently ignoring Brooklyn's rule number four: TAKE A HINT! But it was hard to tell what had happened between us. Maybe Beckett was too cool to cut our date off in a respectable way. After leading me on, he'd made a spectacle and then acted as though he'd been roofied. I was only twenty-four but already over dating games. My domestic future was looking bleak.

"Need a drink, sweetheart?" came the bartender's voice. I focused my attention on the bottles of alcohol.

The only available stool was next to the guy Beckett had said was wasted. He was now slumped pathetically in the same stool he had been in earlier. I pulled the seat out and noticed the guy stiffen as I moved around to sit.

"Something strong," I said to the male bartender.

I had been in that bar enough times to know it was the kind of place where you could say, "Something strong," and the bartender would pour two ounces of Basil Hayden's into a highball glass, and then slide it across the oak. The barstools were cracked and ripped, red vinyl that no one had bothered replacing in thirty years, but the bar top was meticulously polished to perfection every night. It's called *knowing what's important* when you own a dive bar.

I sipped the bourbon and glanced at the drunken man to my right. He didn't look particularly wasted. He was looking at me out of the corner of his eye, his expression was one of moderate fear. I watched his Adam's apple bob as he swallowed. I swiveled my stool so that my entire body was facing him. He continued facing forward, his posture rigid.

"Hello." I was not a particularly social person, but I was intrigued by the strange comment he had made to Beckett earlier and by his bizarre music choices.

He turned only his head toward me, slowly, with painful caution and mouthed, "Oh shit."

My eyes locked with his. I leaned in a fraction of an inch. *Is that possible?* Was it possible for a person to have hair that dark and eyes the color of blue phosphate, like a glacial depth with no end and no beginning? His hair was a longish mess combed back by his black Wayfarer sunglasses sitting askew atop his head. His lips were full and parted enough that I could tell he was breathing in and out through his mouth, his chest heaving. He was wearing a black T-shirt, black pants, and black boots. His face was all narrow sharp angles with two or three days of growth.

"Hello," he said wearily.

He smelled faintly of Mentholatum and baby powder, as though somehow his breath, although completely pleasant, was thicker than air. Everything about him was intoxicating. I was already intoxicated enough.

I stuck out my hand. "I'm Evey."

Without moving his body a smidge, he glanced at my hand and stared at it long enough to make me uncomfortable, and then suddenly his eyes were back on mine.

"Lucian," he said, offering his name but still refusing contact.

"You a germophobe or something, Lucian?"

"Yes," he whispered, absently as his eyes stayed fixated on my lips.

"My friend who I was with earlier said you were wasted. You don't seem wasted to me."

He jerked his head back and scrunched his eyebrows together as if I had wounded him.

The bartender interrupted. "Oh, I assure you, he's thoroughly sauced. He's had a fifth of Jameson in two hours. I'm about to cut him off."

"One more," Lucian said, pushing his empty glass across the bar. His voice was silky warm. He showed no signs that the alcohol had affected him.

The bartender opened a new bottle, arched his eyebrows, and said, "Same as before?"

"Please," Lucian said.

"Okay, man. I don't know how you're doing it, but you're not causing trouble, so I guess it's your call."

"Thank you," Lucian said as the bartender filled the entire tumbler up to the top with brown liquid. My eyes went wide as Lucian lifted the glass to his beautiful mouth and took four large gulps.

"Jesus Christ!" I mumbled.

He turned back toward me, startled. "Where?" He didn't sound angry but surprised.

"Nothing." I felt strangely comfortable next to him but equally tongue-tied.

I didn't think I had ever met a guy so uniquely good-looking. He could have been a print model, but his teeth were slightly imperfect. I looked down his long, lean body and tried to picture what was underneath his clothes. He swallowed nervously, and I realized I was making him uncomfortable.

"This place is pretty old," I said, trying to make conversation.

"I like old," he replied.

"Well, if you're worried about my germs, I'd consider this bar top and the dirty rag Chewbacca has been using to wipe it down."

Lucian didn't flinch. He glanced at my mouth like he was about to kiss me. "You've had a lot to drink tonight."

Pointing at his chest and smiling, I said, "Pot," then I pointed at mine and said, "kettle."

He laughed, and I liked the sound of it. It was contagious.

"You got me," he said.

"So, tell me why you really wouldn't shake my hand?"

He stopped laughing, straightened his body, put his glass

up, and drank the entire contents of it. This guy could put 'em away.

"Last one, I promise," he said, pushing the glass back across the bar. This time, he did sound slightly affected by the alcohol.

The bartender shook his head but filled Lucian's glass anyway, then he looked at me and said, "Will you vouch for me if this guy drops dead?"

"I'm as shocked as you are," I told him.

Lucian ignored us, took a sip, set down the glass, swiveled his stool in my direction and stuck out his hand. "You're right." His voice was rougher, looser from the drink. "I was rude before. I'm Lucian. It's nice to meet you."

When his hand met mine, there was a spark of static electricity. We both pulled back.

"Ouch," I squeaked.

He laughed. "Sorry, try again?"

His hand was warm and smooth. I felt energy in his grasp, almost like the warmth from our connected hands had begun traveling up my arm. I looked at my arm in disbelief just before Lucian yanked his hand back.

"That was weird," I said.

"Uh-huh." He was searching my eyes.

"Now tell my why you said 'oh shit' when you first saw me," I said, my confidence growing with every sip of my bourbon. A high, deep dimple appeared on his right cheek. It was the only way I could tell he was smirking. "Well?" I pushed.

His mouth flattened; he took a gulp of whiskey and then set down his glass. Our eyes locked. "I said it because I was awestruck by your beauty." He was starting to slur, but he still had an elegance about him. Something in his mannerisms was mature for his age and refined, not a typical barfly slugging whiskey after midnight in a dive.

"Oh," was all I could think to say.

Facing forward, he put his attention back on his drink. When he spoke again, he didn't turn to look at me. It was as though he was talking to no one at all. "You should call it a night, Evelyn."

"Excuse me?" I hadn't told him my name was Evelyn, but I assumed one could guess what Evey would be short for.

Yanking a wallet from his back pocket, he said to the bartender, "Close us out, please."

When he threw his American Express across the bar, my jaw dropped to the floor. "Oh, I'm sorry, do we know each other? Do you actually think I'm going to leave with you?"

He finished all of his whiskey then picked up mine and finished that as well.

"Hey!" I said. "What do you think you're doing?" After a moment, he stood and faced me, wobbling and squinting, trying to focus. "It's finally catching up with you, isn't it? You're tossed, man."

He laughed. "Yeah, I am. Shit." He held the bar with his right hand, anchoring himself while he signed his receipt with his left. He was very obviously swaying now. "I'm going to use the restroom," he slurred.

When he stumbled away, Han Solo said, "That guy is gonna die... seriously. You don't understand how much he's had to drink."

"Maybe I should see if he wants me to call someone for him?"

"Yeah, like an ambulance," he shot back.

"Listen, Han, you were the one who should have cut him off." I scowled, but Han was watching something behind me. Before I could turn around, Lucian's hand was on my shoulder. "Mmm." I closed my eyes. Then I jerked up straight. "Oh my God, did I just do that?"

The bartender nodded, trying to stifle a laugh.

Lucian released his hand from my shoulder, so I swiveled around quickly to look at him. "Do you want me to call someone for you, Lucian? Like a friend or family member? You seem really drunk."

He shook his head, closed his eyes, and swayed as though he was going to fall down. "I'm going to walk you home. You live close by."

Peculiarly, I was touched by this mysterious and handsome drunk. "How do you know where I live? My house could be ten miles away. Maybe I took a cab here?"

"Because I noticed that you left earlier and came back. I just figured you lived close by. You look familiar, like I've seen you in the neighborhood."

I knew I had never seen him. No woman could forget a face like his. "I don't know if I need an escort, but thank you. I might stay and have another drink."

"Not a good idea, Evey. You hate hangovers."

"Do I?" I arched my eyebrows. He was so drunk he was acting as though we knew each other. It was comical and a little creepy.

"Well, everyone hates hangovers."

"True, and you are going to have quite the hangover tomorrow, buddy. I don't think you need to worry too much about me."

He squinted and smiled faintly, like he had found some

kind of ironic humor in my comment. We were staring at each other silently, with this unusual sense of knowing and attraction that I didn't understand.

Chewbacca walked by and said in a non-Wookiee voice, "He's harmless. Even if he had bad intentions, do you really think he could pull it off? Look at him."

"Okay, well, listen for my screams. I only live a couple of blocks away."

When I looked back at Lucian, his eyes were closed and he was swaying again. I should have been more scared of him, but I wasn't. I got up to leave, and like a puppy dog, Lucian followed me without a word. Out on the street, he took my hand as though he needed me to guide him while he shuffled along a step behind me.

"I think I'm doing more of the 'walking someone home' than you are." I could still feel the comforting warmth and strange magnetism in his hand.

"You see me, I'm always here," was all he said.

"At that bar? No, I've never seen you there before, and I've been there at least ten times."

"Right," he agreed, closing his eyes again.

"Don't pass out on me." When we reached my building, I waited for him to say something, but he didn't. "This is me. I gotta go. Do you know where you are?"

"Yeah, I'm at your building," he slurred. He kept blinking, trying to focus. "I'm okay. You can go." He nodded toward the door. "Go ahead."

"Okay, bye... be safe," I called back. While I unlocked the door from the street leading into our building, I turned and noticed he was still watching me.

"I'll wait until you're in," he said.

At that point, it had already been the single most bizarre night of my life.

2

TRUTH

Lucian

JUST GO IN, Evelyn. Quit looking back. Forget what I look like.

Zack is always talking about the rules. "They exist for a reason," he likes to say, though none of us actually know what the reasons are. I was currently breaching too many of *the rules* to count. Plus I was drunk again and a hundred percent sure I was going to hear about it from Mona as soon as the night was over.

Just before Evelyn entered the building, she turned back to me and said, "Do you want to come up... sleep it off on the couch? My roommate is probably home so..."

She was saying her roommate was home so I wouldn't think she wanted to sleep with me. *So transparent,*

Evelyn, really!

I thought about what it would be like to sleep with Evey. I thought about touching every inch of her body and running my hands through her brown hair, getting lost in her brown eyes... being inside of her... her warmth.

I shook my head, trying to displace the thoughts of her naked body... in my arms. Such a beautiful woman Evelyn had become. "No, I can't."

"How far is your place?" she asked.

"Just up the way, a couple of blocks." I was beginning to sober up.

"You don't want to come up for coffee or something?" she asked again, her expression hopeful.

I waited for a moment, listening for something—Mona, my conscience, God, anything—but there was nothing. "Okay fine."

I was well aware that I was making a huge mistake. I couldn't disappoint her though. Not when the two us were seeing each other... finally.

Zack's first rule and most commonly talked about was: never show them who you really are.

She motioned for me to go inside. Once I was in the entryway of the building, I stopped and waited for her to lead the way up the stairs.

"You okay?" she said, passing me in the stairwell.

I cleared my throat. "Yes."

"You're about to puke, huh?"

"No. I'm okay."

Once inside the apartment, she stopped at the kitchen. "I'll grab you a water. The living room is down there." She pointed me in the right direction.

I walked to the living room and flipped on the light. The apartment was empty. The pigsty adjacent to the living room—otherwise known as Brooklyn's room—was also eerily quiet.

"No one is here," I called out.

Evey walked up holding a glass of water. "Sit down. My roommate should be home soon."

I took the glass and sat on the couch. "Thank you."

When I glanced out of the window, I saw Zack on the stoop across from Evey's building. He was glaring at me, making a neck-slicing motion with his hand.

"Fuck," I said, watching him.

"What are you looking at?" Evey asked as she sat on the couch as far away from me as she could.

I turned my entire body toward her. "Evelyn, I want to tell you something."

"Okay."

"I'm an angel." I didn't know what came over me, but being there, in plain view, made me feel like purging two thousand years of pent-up frustration.

She didn't hesitate. "You seem sweet. I know you've had a lot to drink, but I'm not worried."

"Well, you should be, dammit. Honestly, Evelyn, inviting a drunk stranger up to your apartment at two a.m.? I'm appalled."

"What? You don't seem drunk anymore."

To my relief, she was finally showing some signs of fear and self-preservation by stiffening her body and moving farther away from me. At that point, she was hugging the arm of the chair like she was about to jump up and bolt.

"I'm an actual angel. I'm not saying I'm sweet, although

I'd argue..." I waved my hand around, vaguely. "Never mind."

Her mouth was turning up into a smile. She stood cautiously and started to back away from the couch. In a really sweet voice, wearing a kind smile, she said, "Have you been to see a doctor, or maybe spent time in treatment?"

"What are you talking about, like rehab?" I mean, I knew I had been drinking a lot but...

"Um, um, psychiatric," she said, softly.

"You're kidding. I finally tell someone, and they don't even believe me." I stood from the couch, a bit wobbly, and took a deep breath. Being free finally did feel amazing, but I wanted her to believe me. I wanted to tell her everything. I held my arms out and said, "I feel liberated. It feels so good. Really, Evey, I've been carrying that shit around for eons. I'm glad I told you."

She laughed with the frightened kind of hysteria, so I smiled warmly at her. She took three deep breaths, and then her laugh turned into something more amused, like she was talking herself out of being scared.

"Well, won't you get in trouble for outing yourself? I mean, won't God be upset with you for telling me?" Now she was playing along.

"I don't know. I've never met him. He's kind of a private guy, and I've heard he has a temper." I smirked. The truth was that I had no idea what was going to happen to me. I could still see Zack, but now he was outside of Evey's window and miming different versions of a violent death. I pointed toward the window. "Can you see that, Evey?"

She looked outside, and then back at me. "See what?"

"Nothing," I said.

Zack wouldn't have done anything that stupid. After all,

he was the one constantly blabbering about the rules.

"So, Lucian, ha! Great name, except that it sounds a bit like Lucifer."

"He's my cousin and he's an ass, okay? The rumors are true. He's not someone I associate with. Seriously, it's a family name; it means nothing."

Evey buckled over laughing.

"Hypothetically, Evey, say I wasn't a celestial being created for the sole purpose of protecting ungrateful people like yourself, would you think it wise to taunt and tease me? A lunatic you picked up off the street and decided to invite into your apartment?"

"Hypothetically? Oh my gosh, you're killing me. This is actually kind of fun. I'll play along." She sat in a chair near the fireplace and tapped her index finger on her chin. "So how do you know what your orders are if you don't talk to God?"

"I have a liaison named Mona." I looked at the ceiling. "How do I explain it? She's basically like an overpaid consultant."

"Overpaid consultant?" Evey was smiling and nodding, eyebrows arched.

"Uh, more like an overpaid supervisor." What I really wanted to say was that Mona was the bane of my existence, a controlling, condescending bitch.

"Interesting," Evey said, her voice laced with sarcasm. "What is she paid in... gold halos?"

I rolled my eyes. "No, she's paid in money, silly. Have you not learned anything about the way the world works? I thought I taught you better than this."

"Okay, so your consultant gives you advice on how

to be an angel?"

"Something like that. She's supposed to convey and interpret information. She's a messenger, like a bike messenger, but high maintenance and obnoxious and not as athletic."

"I see, so she's the messenger kind of angel. What does that make you? Are you an archangel or something?"

"Do you really think I'd be drinking myself to death in shitty bars and sitting in your apartment having a redundant conversation if I were an archangel?"

She laughed. "I'm sorry I'm boring you. Why haven't you told anyone until now?"

"Well, you know..." I smiled and opened my eyes wide. "You know, Evey. Come on?"

She shook her head, looking around. "What? No, I've no clue."

"You know I could be sent"—I pointed at the floor and whispered—"down there."

"Oh, I see. To burn in the fiery depths of hell for an eternity with your cousin Lucifer?"

"Yes, exactly."

"So there is a hell?"

"I can't be sure, but who would want to risk it?"

"This is fun, Lucian. You have quite the imagination. My life is complete now. I've met an angel who sits in bars, binge drinking and playing stupid songs on the jukebox."

I chuckled. "I was bored. This is the second-most boring job in the universe, especially since I started following your ass around."

"What's the first? Wait a minute, did you say following my ass around?"

"The first most mind-numbingly boring job is being God of course. You've created everything"—I waved my hand back and forth, gesturing around the room—"so you know how it's all gonna end. What's the fun in that?" I shrugged. "Oh, and I follow you around because I'm a guardian angel. I'm *your* guardian angel."

Now Zack was hanging from an imaginary noose outside the window.

For a moment, it looked as though Evey was thinking about something serious, like perhaps she believed what I was saying or at least considering it, but then she laughed sarcastically. "So am I your only one?"

"You mean pain in the ass? Yeah, you're the only one. They've been giving me a light caseload lately." I shook my head, still in disbelief that my centuries of fucking penance hadn't gotten me off probation.

"Why is that?"

"Nothing." I didn't feel like sharing my stupidity with her at the moment.

"Tell me, I'm dying to know."

"Are you really dying, Evey? I'm very literal." I shook my head. "I know you're being sarcastic, so I'll keep my career woes to myself, thank you very much."

Her expression softened. "I'm actually curious to hear what you'll come up with."

"It wasn't even my fault. One of my souls—Joan." I sucked air in through my teeth. "It didn't end so well. I had too many to handle at the time. I did fail her, but in my defense, she was an even bigger pain in the ass than you are. Now I'm on a probationary status, which makes an already boring job barely tolerable."

"I'm totally appreciating your quick wit even though I know you're completely full of shit. So this Joan woman, what happened?"

"It was a long time ago. She kept going over my head." Even I was beginning to find humor in what I was telling her.

"Oh, *haha*! That's hysterical. Joan of Arc, I get it. You should write this stuff down. Okay, so how long are you going to keep up the act?"

"It's not an act, and honestly, Evey, I'm a little disappointed in you right now... in your faith and your bad choices tonight," I said, looking pointedly at her.

"You are a strange person. I'm kinda hoping my roommate will come home soon, but you can just leave if you want. How were you wasted an hour ago—you could barely talk or walk—and now you're sitting here making up elaborate stories? I thought you'd pass out the second you hit the couch."

"Oh, well that's easy to explain. My metabolism is a lot faster than yours. I can eat and drink a whole bunch."

"Are you bragging, or are you saying you have some special angel quality that allows you to drink more alcohol?" She smirked.

"I'm not human. I don't sleep—I can't. I wish I could because you bore me to tears and I have to watch over you."

"Uh huh. So you don't sleep, but you get wasted?"

"There's no rule about drinking and flying last time I checked, but I wouldn't be much of a guardian angel if I slept on the job, now would I?"

"You're a bit arrogant and completely insane, but you are definitely creative, I'll give you that. Do your wings sprout out of your shirt when you take flight?"

"No, they're always there. You just can't see 'em."

"I bet they're big, huh?" She rolled her eyes.

"They're huge. Did you see the size of my feet? Thirteens." I pointed at my boots, bit my bottom lip, and wiggled my eyebrows. "All the other angels say size doesn't matter, but wait till you see me in action." I was still a little drunk. I was flirting with her. I was despicable.

"Great, so my guardian angel is a perverted narcissist."

She'd left out that I was a drunk as well, which was a relief.

"Not a pervert, just stating the facts. Anyway"—I stood, took a step back, and waved my arms around—"all of you agnostics want proof, so I'll give it to you."

I was tired of hiding, lying, sneaking. I wanted her to know. I wanted to push the envelope and see if Mona would swoop in and banish me. The truth was that I couldn't watch Evey anymore, not when she was dating, falling in love, hanging out with moronic apes. Mona refused to reassign me—she wouldn't even let me plead my case, so I was done. I had been pushed too far, driven to alcoholism.

Come on, an alcoholic angel? I was a cliché. I hated myself. "I'm not gonna sit here and spew facts about every stage of your colorless, insipid, shallow life that I had to so painfully watch. I'm just not, okay? They always do that in movies, and I think, 'Why not disappear and reappear? What's the deal? We're angels.' I could turn into a fire-breathing dragon right now if I wanted to." She suddenly looked terrified, so I held out my hand. "Don't worry, I'm not going to scare you."

3

LIES

Evelyn

"JUST GONNA POP out…"

He seemed to believe what he was saying. I wondered if he was an actor. And then, like an absolute dream—nope… nightmare—he clapped once and disappeared into thin fucking air.

I gasped. "Oh my God! Oh my God!" I fell to the floor and held my hand over my chest. I was having a heart attack. I was sure of it.

And then he reappeared. "And… pop back in," he said, stumbling to the side. "Shit, I need to work on my reentry."

"Oh God! Oh Lord," I kept chanting.

"No, it's Lucian. Why is everyone so obsessed with that guy?" He looked at me steadily, and then I think he saw the terror in my eyes, finally. "Shit."

Lucian turned into Mrs. Obernickle, my preschool teacher. "Now, dear, don't be scared."

"This is not happening, this is not real. I've been drugged. I'm dreaming. Did you drug me so you could kill me?" I said to Mrs. Obernickle as I stood on shaky legs.

"Oh no, of course not, dear."

As horrifying as the situation was, I found her voice and smell comforting. Still, my heart was beating out of my chest. I looked into her crystal-blue eyes, and I saw him. I whispered, "Lucian?"

He turned back into himself. "You rang?"

I just continued to blink at him until tears flooded my eyes. His expression softened; he braced my shoulders. I was scared at first, and then warmth rushed through my body. My knees buckled, and he swooped me off my feet as if I were as light as a feather. The warm feeling was familiar. He had done that to me before; I just hadn't known it at the time.

I remembered once, when my mother forgot to pick me up at school, I had waited in the dark. I was terrified and cold. I started to cry, then that now-familiar warmth filled me. I remembered it because it was strange. When my mom had finally arrived, I told her I thought I had a fever. Lucian holding me in my apartment was a fever dream—it had to be—but I was starting to believe he had been there with me whenever I felt scared or alone.

I felt warm and safe as he carried me effortlessly over to the couch. Without words, he set me down, walked to the kitchen, and returned a moment later with chamomile tea.

"I put honey in it... the way you like it." He smiled, seeming unsure as he handed it over. Then he stood back, took a deep breath, and ran his hand through his longish dark hair.

"Thank you," I said.

"I'm really sorry about that. I just felt so free after telling you, I didn't think about how it would make you feel."

He lifted my legs, sat down and then pulled them up on his lap. He rested his head on the back of the couch and rubbed my shins in soft strokes. Warmth coursed through me the moment he and I made contact. I felt like I was in a bathtub. He closed his eyes and took a deep breath.

After twenty minutes of silence, I felt completely relaxed.

"More tea?" he asked.

I sat up. "Actually I think I want another drink."

"It's late." Something had changed in him. He seemed resigned, but I felt absolutely at ease, even though my brain was still processing the impossible events that had occurred in front of my eyes moments earlier.

"Do you want a little red wine?" he asked.

"Mmhmm, but I don't think I have any."

He took his glass of water and handed it to me. The moment it was in my hand, the water became wine.

"I bet you have a lot more questions?" he said.

"Well, it's not every day..."

"Fire away."

"So you've been watching over me my entire life?"

"Pretty much, yeah."

My eyes shot open. "So you've seen me..."

"Oh no, I don't spy on you. I've never seen you naked. Except that one time." He shook his head. "Never mind."

"Were you Mrs. Obernickle?"

"Not all the time. Only when you cried at school... to

comfort you. For a preschool teacher, she was kind of a cold bitch. God her perfume made me nauseous... still does." He made a weird gagging sound and shook his head. I smiled, and he smiled back. "I liked it better when you were making fun of me and didn't believe a word I said. I'm sorry I scared you, Evey."

"Who else have you been in my life?"

"Um, the old guy you played chess with in the park."

"Charlie? You were Charlie?"

"Only once you started getting good. He wasn't challenging you anymore."

"Ha! So where did you come from? Do you float around? Do you live somewhere?"

"I basically just follow you around. Sometimes when I know you're all right, I take off and do my own thing." His demeanor was sweet, almost shy now. "I followed you home earlier and saw you looking out the window. I thought you were going to bed, but then you showed up at the bar again."

"So why didn't I see you outside?"

He seemed to be pondering what he should tell me. "Did you see the woman walking a little white dog?"

"That was you?"

"Yeah. I'm whoever, whenever I need to be. I got lazy at the bar when you were with that guy. Honestly, Evelyn, that guy?" He scowled. "You were all swept up in him, so I didn't go to great lengths to disguise myself. Not that it would have mattered." His tone was strangely bitter. "We're not supposed to reveal what we really look like to our souls."

"Why?"

"Because we're just not. It's hard to explain."

"Try me."

"Do you know what transference is? Like with patients and doctors?"

"I think I do. So you think that I'd fall in love with you or something because your job is to protect me?" It wouldn't be hard. He smelled delicious, looked incredibly sexy, and his touch was spellbinding.

"I'm created to make you feel comfortable. You must sense that?"

I nodded. "But if you didn't feel the same way..."

"We don't." He went rigid. "We're not made to fall in love."

I glanced at his jeans. He followed my eyes.

"I have average parts," he said quickly, and then his arrogant smile reappeared. "Although I wouldn't actually call mine average, but yes, I have man parts. We can date each other—angels can date each other—but our jobs are too demanding for a serious commitment."

It all sounded so logistical and practical, and honestly, quite comical.

I started feeling dizzy. "Is this really happening?"

He moved quickly and gracefully. "Lie down." He pulled me on top of him. My head was on his shoulder, and he was stroking my hair. He lowered his voice to a warm rumble in his chest. "When you struggle, I come through people in your life. Sometimes when you're alone, I'm here too. I've done this a million times, but I couldn't let you feel my physical body."

Shame. I felt warm and calm in his arms. "Do all angels look like you?"

His chuckle lightened the mood. "No, you just got lucky."

"When do you date?" I asked.

"There's an empty time slot every night based on your geographic location. It's a couple of hours when we have to meet with our supervisor if nothing is happening."

"So we all freeze at midnight or something?"

"For humans, it's one minute, but for us, it's about two hours. Basically your time is slowed down. You're moving, but it's barely detectable. So if there're no real issues and I don't have to meet with Mona, I date a little." He shrugged one shoulder.

"How do you meet potential dates?"

"Tinder."

I sat up quickly. "Stop it."

"I swear. Angels can see other angels' wings, so when a profile pops up, we always know whether to swipe left or right."

When I laughed, he smiled, just before his eyes darted to the ceiling. "Oh shit," he whispered, and then he was gone.

It was jarring. My face hit the couch as Brooklyn's voice came from the front door. "Pinky, you here?"

I'd never told her, but I resented the nickname. After all, I had contracted pink eye after staying the night in her filthy childhood bedroom.

"I'm here," I yelled to Brooklyn. Under my breath, I said, "Lucian, if you're here, give me a sign." There was nothing. No warm feelings, no floating vases, no thunder or lightning in the distance.

Brooklyn came into the living room and threw her coat and purse on the couch next to me. "I thought you'd be here with what's his face?"

"Beckett? No. The date was horrible."

She plopped down on the green velvet chair next to the

fireplace. "I told you it would happen. Only a matter of time."

I sat up and crossed my arms, still shaken up over what I had either hallucinated or experienced moments before. I wasn't going to tell her about Lucian, but I wondered if people knew about angels and didn't talk about it. "Do you believe in guardian angels?"

"No. If I had a guardian angel, do you really think I would have gotten that heinous sunburn last summer in Cabo?"

"How was your night?" I asked.

"Stupid." That meant she hadn't gotten the attention she wanted. "I'm going to bed." She got up and left the room. "Night, Pinky."

I looked around for any sign that Lucian had been there. I picked up the glass from the table. I had drunk all of the wine, but there was still a red ring lining the bottom of the glass. I held it up with triumph and said, "I'm not crazy."

"No one said you were, weirdo!" Brooklyn yelled from her bedroom.

"Good night," I called to her as I got up and headed to my room. Inside my room, I began to undress and then stiffened. "Lucian? If you're here, you have to tell me."

I remembered what he'd said about not spying on me. I slowly undressed, still on edge and shaking. I got into my bed, exhausted but terrified, then I began the prayer I had said every night since I was a child. It had never held any meaning until now. It was always just a habit, a soothing mechanism my mother had taught me.

"Angel of God, my Guardian dear..."

4

PRAYERS

Lucian

STANDING OUTSIDE HER building, I waited until she started the prayer. I could always hear Evey, even in my thoughts. Sometimes it was like static or white noise, and then she would say something out loud that would get my attention, especially when I wasn't with her. When that happened, I would feel a pull, an energy or force bringing me back to her.

A moment later, I was in her room, standing next to her bed. She couldn't see me or hear me, but I was chanting the prayer with her. She was dozing off. Right at the moment that she fell asleep, I put my hand on her shoulder and she smiled faintly.

What the fuck have I done?

I knew Zack would be waiting for me outside. He only

had two souls—a husband and wife in their sixties, who lived across the street from Evey and rarely left their apartment. His assignment was so easy that he actually had time to start an online sports betting ring... lucky bastard. He had something to live for, something of his own. Brooklyn's angel, Abigail, was currently sitting on the stoop, looking at her phone. She was probably on Tinder.

"Idiot," she mumbled as I walked by. Abigail looked like Heidi Klum, but other than that, there was nothing angelic about her.

I ignored her and headed down the block. Angels were everywhere. Most of them had several souls in one area, and most of them spent this time of night minding their own business and waiting for the magic hours to begin, which happened right before sunrise. For sixty seconds before the sun pierced the horizon, angels had two hours of freedom. It was like trying to fit your entire social life into a lunch break. Half the time I'd spend it sitting with Mona, trying to talk my way out of some mess I had gotten into.

Zack appeared beside me. I didn't look over.

"Why are you sneaking up on me, shitbag?" I asked.

He was laughing. "You're in so much trouble. Why are you always in trouble?"

"I haven't done anything serious in fifty years," I told him.

"Oh wow, nothing in fifty whole years? It's been a century since I've even had a warning."

I flew away and headed for Twenty-Fourth Street. During the magic hours, we had to check-in with our overseers before we could take off and have some fun. Zack, two other angels—Lauren and Bob—and I all had to meet with Mona.

We met her at the St. Francis Fountain, a soda shop where Doug worked. Doug didn't have any souls. He'd kept violating his probation, so they banished him to the St. Francis soda shop and hotel. The higher-ups liked to be ironic; it was part of their sick humor. During the day, Doug cleaned hotel rooms, and at night, he worked in the soda shop. He could never leave... ever! There were other angels like Doug who ran establishments during magic hours. I imagined that Mona would sentence me to some type of hell like Doug's, but I was ready for it.

My hell was watching Evey date every guy in the city.

When the magic hours began, I was the first to walk through the jingling door. Doug greeted me. "Hey, Luc, the usual?" He had a secret stash of whiskey under the counter that he'd pour in my coffee.

"Lay off the bottle, you drunk!" came Mona's voice from the corner booth. All I could see was the top of her head, the bright red and perfectly coifed bun popping up over the green vinyl booth back.

I looked at Doug and smiled. "Make it a double."

"You got it." Doug didn't care about pissing off Mona.

I slid into the seat across from her as Doug set my coffee in front of me.

Mona shook her head in disgust. "You know, Lucian, I was thinking... a few of us are getting tired of meeting here. The music is terrible, and honestly, we'd enjoy a drink every now and then too. Doug doesn't spike all of our coffees."

The door jingled. Zack walked in and took a seat at the bar while simultaneously flipping me off.

I put my focus back on Mona. She had the tiniest mouth, pursed red lips, and a pointy ski-slope nose. Impish would be an understatement. "You look nice tonight." I arched my eyebrows and dropped my gaze to her mouth.

She sucked in a breath and held it.

I leaned forward over the table and whispered, "Wanna fuck?"

She swallowed. "Lucian," she said in a warning tone.

"I know you want me. Why don't you live a little?" I lowered my voice. "I want to taste you, Mona, you little tart."

Her face flushed. "Don't. Stop."

"Oh, I don't plan to. Not until you're screaming my name."

"I meant don't say another word."

Since angels didn't age, we were all perpetually in our prime, which meant that even though Mona was centuries older than me, she had all the same feelings that I did. I was getting to her; she wanted me.

"I want to bite your perfect ass," I said.

That did it. That put her over the edge.

She cleared her throat and held up a Wookiee costume from the bench. "How would you like to work at the Star Wars bar for eternity? You'd get to see Evey every weekend with one hipster after another, her heart getting more mangled each time. Maybe we'll reassign her to Abigail."

"No!" I said, banging my hand on the table. I could handle the Star Wars bar for eternity, but I could not handle knowing self-absorbed Abigail would be looking out for Evey. "You have to get her someone better."

"I don't have to do anything. I know what you're doing, Lucian. You're trying to get banished. You want to sabotage yourself because you're some kind of masochist."

"I'm not, Mona. That's the thing." I shrugged. "If I were,

I'd enjoy watching Evey date these cretins she goes out with."

"This is so out of the ordinary. It has to be all the drinking. You're just not thinking clearly. I don't want to have to go to my supervisor with this."

I smacked my hand on the table again.

"Stop doing that!" she said.

I was getting so tired of the cryptic shit. "Who the fuck is your supervisor? Is it him?" I pointed up.

"No, no, of course not. It's David."

"Like as in *the* David?"

"No, a different one. He's just my supervisor," she said.

"Where is the big guy? Let me talk to him."

"You know you can't do that."

I took a deep breath. I felt like I was going to throw up. Zack, Bob, and Lauren were all at the bar now, eavesdropping. I motioned for Mona to lean in over the table so I could whisper to her.

She rolled her eyes. "I'm not falling for that one. You're so arrogant."

"Please, I'm serious," I pleaded.

She huffed then finally leaned over the table toward me.

I cupped her ear. "I'm in love with her," I whispered.

She yanked her head back and scowled. "With who?"

I mouthed, "Evey."

"That's impossible. She's human. You don't even have the chemicals in your body to be attracted to her."

All three angels at the bar turned on their stools and stared at me with wide eyes.

I stood abruptly. "Oh, fuck all of you. You don't understand." I rushed out of the door and took off toward the sky.

We couldn't actually breathe outside of the atmosphere, so as soon as I hit about ten thousand feet, I started gasping and choking—plus I was freezing my ass off. I just had to get away. Nothing made sense. We were living and breathing just like Evey. I had a heart that beat. I could smell and taste and touch just like Evey. I came barreling back toward the ground, landed in the same spot I'd taken off from, and stumbled to my left. Zack was sitting outside the soda shop, watching me.

"What happened to you? You used to be so good at that," he said.

"Everything is turning to shit." I sat down next to him at the curb. "What did Mona say after I left?"

"She thinks it's the drinking."

I looked at Zack; he had strawberry-blond hair, freckles, and a boyish face. He was my best friend, and half the time I knew he was looking out for me. The other half of the time, he was heckling me. We were like brothers. He was the closest thing, besides Evey, that I had to family.

"What's eating you, man? And why'd you tell Evey? You know what you're gonna have to do now, right?"

"I know."

I had to erase Evey's memory of me. We didn't like to do that often because occasionally it caused forgetfulness—a response to the energy we forced into the brain. We did it by pressing a thumb to the forehead and funneling the electrical currents in our body out through the fingers. If you did it right, you could go on unseen, and your soul would just pick up where they'd left off.

"You should do it soon—before she starts talking. They'll have her committed."

"I will, first thing after we go back."

Angels had gifts. Obviously we could use other physical bodies, we had invisible wings, and we were generally more efficient beings. Our hearts were faster, we could eat and drink more, and though we were ageless, we weren't immortal. We weren't susceptible to diseases or age-related illnesses, but we could still die by getting hit by a truck. At the instant of our death, we'd just disintegrate into nothing and immediately be forgotten. What a legacy.

One thing about my job that had been bugging me for a century at least was that we were kept in the dark from all the higher-ups. We had been created and predisposed to protect our souls, but the rules, especially Zack's long list of rules, came from hearsay. Mona acted as a lawyer in a way. She would interpret information from the higher-ups then try to apply it to our situations, but I didn't think she could prove that me being in love with Evey was impossible.

I didn't know what was happening to me. I had heard stories of angels falling in love with their souls, but I'd never heard about what had eventually happened to them.

"Remember Connie? That one that fell in love with the musician?"

"Yeah, I remember," I said.

"It wasn't that long ago," Zack added.

We had all heard this story about an angel in Memphis who had fallen in love with her assigned soul, but the guy died. That was the end of it.

"He's one of us now."

"What?"

"Yeah, in New York. Connie took him out herself."

"What? Why? How?"

"So they could be together."

"I'm confused."

He turned his body toward me. "I know how to fix your situation with Evey. If I tell you, will you teach me that trick?"

Zack had been hassling me about the same stupid trick for a hundred years. Literally... a hundred years.

"I'll try, but it takes a pretty strong set to pull it off." I glanced at his pathetic wings, all dry, brownish-red, and sparse-feathered.

"I can do it," he said.

"Fine." I stood. "Let's get a bottle first."

He rolled his eyes. We headed back to Evey's street while we downed a bottle of Glenfiddich. We still had about an hour left.

"Okay, show me the trick now," Zack said once we were in front of Evey's building.

He wanted to know how to do a three-sixty loop. You fly fast up and flip back around, but it's really only cool if you have grace. Zack could barely fly straight. But I'd said I would teach him.

"Tell me your secret first." We flew up to sit outside of Evey's window and finish the bottle. I was sauced again for the third time in less than twenty-four hours.

"You have to kill her."

"Excuse me, what?"

"That's what happened to Connie and Jeff. She drowned him in the Mississippi, and he happily went along with it just to be with her. Now that is a love story, man. I guess they're angels in New York City on the same block."

I shook my head. "It's a myth. It has to be."

"No, seriously, that's how we're made. We were all human once, then we got killed. Some of us come here, some go to other places, but we all get jobs in a way. They got lucky that they ended up in the same place. But it's true—we were all human and we all definitely got axed before our time. I know that for sure." He made a slicing motion across his neck.

"I don't believe you. I think I have to kill myself to be with her."

"Nah... you got that from a movie. You can't be with Evey now, the way you are. You'll start dying, really slow and painful. Like each time you get with her, you'll die a little, and then all of the sudden, lights out. When we die, that's it, man. Poof! We're gone. You've seen it?"

I had seen it. I once saw an angel get shot. It's as if we disintegrate into a powdery dust and that's it. Any humans who witness it, instantly forget that we even existed. It's really depressing.

"Why would I die from being with Evey? Wouldn't I just get banished?"

He looked thoughtful for once. He pitied me. "I don't know. It's just what I heard, okay? I'm not totally sure. You should talk to Mona." He shrugged. "I could be wrong."

I was staring through the window, wondering how I would ever be able to kill Evey. Even if what Zack said was true, how would Evey know she truly wanted to be with me when I was basically made for her comfort? It wouldn't be fair to her.

"Isn't it kind of weird that you want her when you've been watching over her since she was a baby?"

"What are you saying, dick?"

"You know what I'm saying," he said.

"Fuck you. It's not like that. She's beautiful and amazing and kind. I trust her implicitly." I drank the rest of the bottle in three large gulps. "There's no one like her. And she's an adult."

"You're like, two thousand years older than her. You're taking 'robbing the cradle' to a whole new level, man."

"Not exactly two thousand years," I mumbled.

"I told you what you have to do."

"Kill her?" I shook my head. "I could never hurt her. Never."

"Well then, you better learn to accept your fate, buddy. Start following the rules unless you want to be schlepping drinks, dressed like a Wookiee until the sun explodes."

We laughed then, full belly laughs until tears were pouring from my eyes. I imitated a Wookiee sound.

"Good, you're practicing. Now show me that flip," Zack said.

I looked at my watch; we only had about five minutes left. We were both pretty drunk, and I was not in any shape to be doing aerobatic stunts. I stood anyway, set my wings out wide, and flew straight up. I arched my back, flipped, and a second later, everything was black.

5

DREAMS

Evelyn

I WOKE UP trying to figure out if the whole night had been a drug-induced dream. "Lucian," I whispered, and there was nothing. *Someone had to have drugged me.*

It was a Saturday. I had planned to go for a run then work on a few designs for Tracey's stupid denim line. Before I left, I peeked into Brooklyn's mess of a room and spotted her lying on her stomach on top of a pile of dirty clothes strewn across her bed. She was sound asleep and drooling, and her room smelled faintly of bad breath and old pizza. I smiled.

After shutting the door quietly, I jogged down the stairs, feeling unusually good for having been drugged the night before. I wondered if Beckett, that freak, had slipped me something or if it had all just been a vivid dream. I smiled and laughed out loud. It had to have been a dream. Having a sexy guardian angel that I wanted to get naked with was just too good to be true. Then on my way down the steps outside of my building, I stepped on him.

Yep, I stepped on my guardian angel, and he groaned. He was lying on the concrete, facedown. Someone had stuck a piece of cardboard over him as if he was a homeless person. When I pulled the cardboard away, he turned and looked up at me through squinted, swollen eyes. I gasped when I noticed his face was bruised and bloodied.

"Lucian!" I got on my knees.

"I'm okay, Evey," he mumbled. "I drank too much and had a little collision with the side of your building."

He sat up slowly, holding a hand to his head. When he tried to stand, he swayed to one side. I hitched an arm around his waist and led him back up the stoop.

"Come up to my apartment, and I'll clean your face," I said, and then something occurred to me. I looked at him pointedly. "Did you drug me last night?"

"Of course not. I made you tea... so ungrateful." He huffed, shaking his head, and then grimaced and held his free hand to his neck.

"You're a mess. I'm trying to understand how a celestial being with magical

powers, assigned to protect me, is a drunk who runs into the sides of buildings. This doesn't bode well for my future."

"Such a smartass, Evey, really. I technically *flew* into the side of your building, but that's neither here nor there. Zack wanted me to show him a trick. You were sound asleep and safe. I threw caution to the wind."

"Who is Zack? And I have a feeling you were throwing

back a hell of a lot more than just caution."

"You're right, a bottle of whiskey—single malt Scotch to be exact—and Zack is my best friend. He's an angel too."

"So you guys got trashed and decided to fly into walls?"

Lucian sighed the way a person does when they're just too tired to explain themselves. I helped him up the stairs then led him to my bedroom, hoping Brooklyn wouldn't notice.

He sat on the edge of my bed and held his hands to his stomach. "I know I broke some ribs, but I heal fast, so don't worry about me, okay?"

He must have seen the concern on my face. He looked messed up. His hair was going in every direction, there was dried blood on his face, and his lip was split and bleeding. I touched my thumb to his lip and wiped the blood away. He looked up at me, squinting. We were frozen for a moment, staring at each other. There was reverence in his eyes, the same as what I felt for him.

"Thank you," he whispered.

I looked down at my thumb and watched the blood fade, like it was being absorbed into my skin.

"I'll get a warm washcloth," I said before scurrying off to the bathroom. In the bathroom, I stared into the mirror. *Is this really happening?* I shook my head, took a deep breath, and then busied myself getting a washcloth and a cup of water before returning to the room.

He took the water and smelled it. "Do you have anything stronger?"

"Really? Can't you just zap that and turn it into wine like you did before?"

"Only wine. You-know-who stole that idea from me, by

the way. But it's complicated. I can only do it for other people."

"Maybe you should just drink the water. It looks like you could use it." I wiped the blood from his forehead and cheek with the cloth.

He closed his eyes. "Mmm, that feels good. Thank you." He swallowed, looking hesitant. "I have another injury, but I don't want to scare you."

"What is it?"

He looked into his lap at his trembling hands, and then suddenly, swoosh... behind him, the most beautiful set of large black wings extended from the sides of his back. He squeezed his eyes closed.

"Oh my God, they're beautiful." I stumbled back in awe, holding my hand to my chest.

They weren't what I expected. The wings were large, thick, shiny, and black. On his left side, a drop of blood fell from a cluster of feathers at the base of the wing. Lucian inched the wing back in toward his body as he winced, his face scrunching up in pain.

"Wait, let me clean it," I said.

His head drooped, and his shoulders slouched in such a defeated way that it made me cry. Seeing his shame saddened me, and my tears fell onto his feathers as I brushed them with the cloth. Lucian sagged even further into himself.

"When you feel pain, Evey, so do I." I thought it must work exactly the same way for me. "Please don't hurt for me," he said softly.

I swallowed hard, trying to regain control. When I was through cleaning the blood, he closed the wings and they were gone. I felt around his back, but he shook his head.

"You won't be able to feel them unless I want you to, and right now, I just want to lie down and rest."

"I thought you didn't sleep?"

"I don't, but if I rest, I'll heal quicker. Will you do that with me? Rest with me?"

"Yes, of course." I would have done anything he asked. I had the distinct sense that he wasn't able to rest unless I did. I kicked off my running shoes, climbed up to the head of the bed, and propped myself on the pillows. I patted my chest. "I'll hold you."

He looked tortured, but he climbed up the bed with me anyway, laid his head on my chest, and closed his eyes. "I'm supposed to do this for you," he said quietly.

"We can do it for each other."

"You don't understand." He sighed.

He was right—I didn't understand what was happening. I didn't know if I was crazy, dreaming, or dead, but something about Lucian, about the way he smelled and spoke, put me at ease. I should have felt scared, but I wasn't. I wanted to ask Brooklyn to come into my room to see if he was real, but I was afraid he'd leave and I didn't want him to leave... ever. I fell asleep almost instantly to the rhythm of his breaths.

When I woke up, he was no longer lying with me. He was standing above me, next to my bed, looking gloriously handsome and clean.

"Did you shower?" I asked.

He smiled, lifting his index finger to his mouth. "Shh."

Something had changed in his demeanor. There was resignation and surrender, and when I looked closely into his squinting eyes, I also saw veneration... serenity... love. I can't explain what exactly I saw, just that I could feel all of the feelings that he had for me by simply looking at him.

"I'll always be here for you, Evey," he whispered. Then he pressed his thumb to my forehead.

"PINKY!" BROOKLYN YELLED from the other room. "I made pancakes. Come and eat."

Brooklyn loved to cook, but when she did, she made a huge mess and then she would just leave it. I went into the kitchen feeling groggy. Sitting at the small round table in the corner, I scanned the countertops littered with bowls, plates, eggshells, a milk carton, and trash. I rolled my eyes. Brooklyn was playing the song "Clouds" by the Borns loudly from the iPod dock while she danced around flipping pancakes. Not a care in the world.

"Last night was weird, huh?" she yelled over the music.

I put two pancakes on a plate and drizzled syrup over them. "Yeah! Can you turn it down?" I had a vague sense of déjà vu.

Brooklyn turned down the music. "So what happened with Beckett, and why were you acting all creepy weird in the living room by yourself last night?"

What was she talking about? "I wasn't acting weird. Beckett got into this stupid music playing at the Star Wars bar. I think he had them turn it up or something, I don't know. I just left him there and then felt bad about it, so I went back and he was gone. I sat at the bar and had one more drink, alone, before coming back home. Uneventful."

She turned around and smiled. "Whatever you say. You were acting weird."

The details from the night before were a bit foggy, and this morning was even foggier. "Why are you cooking pancakes at two p.m.?"

"Well, because we both slept in and pancakes are yummy," she squealed.

"I think I was headed out for a run, then I went back to sleep. Ugh, I have a headache. I drank too much last night." My head was pounding. I was staring into the open refrigerator.

"What are you looking for?" Brooklyn asked.

"OJ."

"Uh, it's right in front of your face, weirdo."

It was centered in front, on the top shelf.

"Oh."

She knocked lightly on my head. "Hello? Yeah, last night you were even more out of it. Weird how you were like, 'Do you believe in guardian angels?' Um, okay, Pinky, what'd you and Beckett smoke?"

"Guardian angels?" I stood there, stunned, holding a box of orange juice in the middle of the kitchen.

An image of a man popped into my mind, a beautiful man with striking blue eyes and dark hair. I blinked, trying to recall where the image came from. Was it a dream?

6

REGRETS
Lucian

"YOU FUCKED UP," Zack said, appearing beside me in Evey's kitchen as we watched the disaster unfold. "You didn't zap her good enough."

"No, I did."

"Look, I can tell she's thinking about you. If you had zapped her good enough—oh, fuck yeah," Zack mumbled as he looked at his phone. "My wide receiver scored eighteen points today. I'm killin' it like a boss!"

He had zero attention span from all the screen time and video games. I glanced at him. "Is that your sports betting thing?"

"No, moron, it's fantasy football."

Evey and Brooklyn were sitting at the table, eating

pancakes and chatting about some new guys Brooklyn had met. I rolled my eyes and tried to ignore them while Zack and I sat on the counter undetected.

"Dude, get off your phone and talk to me. Isn't that why you're here?" I asked.

Still staring at his screen, he said, "No, I'm here because your weird life is entertaining to me. You know what I think you need? A hobby. You have one soul, and that's why you're losing your shit. You need to do something for Lucian, for yourself."

"Like what?"

"I don't know. Maybe knitting. You can't make one person the center of your universe. You'll go crazy all cooped up in here. Get a hobby. Take up craft-beer making or join a book club."

I was trying to ignore Zack as I watched Evey inhale her pancakes. I zeroed in on a drop of syrup next to her mouth. I wanted to lick it off.

"I zapped her good," I said mindlessly. "I don't know why she's short-circuiting over it."

"Apparently you didn't. You have to hold your thumb down until you smell something burning."

I turned to face him, my jaw on the floor. "Are you kidding me? Is that what you do? You're frying people; you know that, right? It affects them."

He shrugged. "Not really."

"Yeah, really, it does. I can't believe I'm the one who's always in trouble. Anyway, shouldn't you go check in with your souls?"

"They're fine. They're eating and binge watching *Top Chef*."

I believed that their behavior was a direct result of Zack frying them every time he slipped up. Those people ate and watched TV all day and never left their house. But I was the immoral one?

I directed my attention back to Brooklyn and Evey's conversation when I caught Brooklyn saying, "Well, you can get a little action tonight and redeem yourself. You're going out with us. Joel is bringing Keith, and he's gorgeous."

"I feel like I'm gonna puke," I told Zack.

"See, you need a hobby. Want to start a blog? Let's start a blog, dude."

"No," I said, watching Evey agree to go out with Brooklyn. "Geez, for the love of God! These girls can't stay home and read a book?"

"They're young and hot," Zack said.

"Stop, please."

"Gotta go," he said, and then he was gone.

I followed Evey into her bedroom, not something I normally did. She plopped onto her bed, blew her long brown hair out of her face, and stared at the ceiling.

"Guardian angels," she whispered, shook her head and rolled to her side.

I wished I knew what she was thinking. I saw her smell the pillow where I had been lying earlier. She smiled faintly while moving her hand down below, between her legs.

Oh God. Heaven help me now.

I blinked and found myself out on the stoop, sitting next to a derisive Mona.

"Lucian, Lucian, Lucian. You think I don't know what's going on?"

"I know you do. I can't control what's happening to me.

Please, Mona, reassign me. You have to before I do something awful." I was begging now.

"You'll never see her again. I'll send you off to Sarmi first thing tomorrow. Not too many angels can speak Liki as well as you can."

"Well, that's true—I am very good at a lot of things." I smirked. "Please, you have to keep me here. Reassign me? I'll stay away from her, I promise." I knew I couldn't though.

"'I'll stay away from her'? Oh please. It's obvious you're full of shit. Give it another week. I hope you start making better decisions. And Lucian... you didn't zap her well enough," she said, before disappearing.

"Wait, Mona, come back."

I got a bottle of whiskey and sat out on the stoop for hours, just staring off into space. Abigail was sitting next to me, ignoring me as per usual.

She finally looked up from her phone and said, "Hey, I know I've never asked you this before, but will you cover my shift tonight, since they'll be together and what's her name is your only one?"

I shook my head and sighed. "First of all, we are not fucking waiters. We don't cover each other's shifts. And second of all, her name is Evelyn. I think you know that."

She made an ugly-bitch face. "Ew, your breath stinks. You're such an asshole drunk, Lucian. Get a life."

I could hear Evey and Brooklyn talking about getting ready to go out. It was getting dark. I thought about Abigail's offer and wondered if I could use it to my advantage "What's in it for me?"

She shrugged. "I'll give you a blow job?"

"I don't want your disgusting mouth anywhere near me."

She rolled her eyes. "Okay fine. I won't play eyes and ears for Mona anymore."

"Excuse me, what? What are you talking about?"

"Who do you think I'm texting all day? I pick up extra cash as an informant."

"Seriously, an informant?" I threw open my arms and wings. My anger was boiling over. "You're all fucking shameless."

"If it weren't for me watching you watching her getting off from the smell of you—which, by the way, is seriously gross—Mona never would have swooped in to save your ass. You would have regretted it, perv."

I suddenly felt very resolute. "Abigail, I will cover your 'shift' every Saturday night for a year,"—I held up air quotes when I said the word shift—"but you have to promise me something."

"What?" she said.

"No more snooping around, no more telling Mona things, and no more shit-talking to me." I lowered my voice. "We can help each other, okay?"

Before that night, I'd had no idea that was how Mona found things out. I guess you could do a job for two centuries and still be in the dark.

Abigail appeared to be contemplating my offer. "Fine."

When I overheard Evey talking to Brooklyn about a lace thong, I took a swig of whiskey and tried to focus on Abigail. "What plans do you have anyway, if we're all working?"

"I'm seeing someone, and he gets his shifts covered too."

I snickered. "We're not supposed to make commitments to each other. Don't you know that?"

"You and I just made a commitment, didn't we? Anyway,

I wouldn't start talking to me about the rules if I were you. At least I'm dating one of us. Something is off in you for even being attracted to what's her face."

"It's Evelyn, and piss off, Abigail. Go, I'll take it from here. You're free to go see your man."

"Angel," she corrected, before disappearing. She had to get in one final dig.

A second later, Zack swooped over from across the street, flapping his shitty wings. "She is such a stuck-up bitch." He hated the pretty ones because they never gave him the time of day.

"Whatever. She's helping me out."

"Helping you do what?"

"I'm not zapping Evey again. I don't want to mess with her anymore. Did you know that Abigail tells Mona shit?"

Zack didn't respond for several seconds. "Yeah, I mean, I guess I knew."

"Do you tell Mona stuff?" I asked, narrowing my eyes.

"No, don't even go there, bro. I would never."

"I gotta go," I said, before drinking the last of the whiskey.

I popped into Evey's kitchen, where she was mixing up margaritas for her and Brooklyn. Evey was dressed to go out, revealing more skin than usual in her black silk shorts-jumper. Her smooth legs were still tan from the summer. She was wearing three-inch platform heels that I knew belonged to Brooklyn. I made a frustrated sound. She startled and turned around as if she'd heard me. She looked through me... thankfully.

"Brooke?" she called.

My heart was racing. Had she heard me?

"Yeah?" Brooklyn said, walking into the kitchen. "Wow, girl, you look amazing. You're totally gonna get some action."

"I don't need action." Evey handed over the margarita and said thoughtfully, "I'm extremely sated at the moment."

"Ew, what were you doing to yourself in there?"

I felt like I should leave, like I was invading her privacy.

"Oh, shut up, you do it all the time. You don't think I hear the buzzing?" Evey asked.

"Who were you thinking about? Huh? Please don't say Beckett."

I was standing right next to Evey, my mouth near her cheek. I was willing her to say my name but at the same time praying she wouldn't.

"No one in particular." She squinted. "Hot guy fantasy."

Say my name. It looked like she was about to form the letter L. I was as close as I could be to her without actually touching her. I tried to smell her, but I couldn't; I tried to breathe her in, but I couldn't.

She shook her head. "I don't know who I was thinking about."

I'm on the other side of life, Evey, existing where death belongs and yearning to be with you. Yearning in brief moments to bring you here, into the darkness. When my thoughts are so painfully selfish, I cannot breathe you in at all. I cannot love you when I hate myself. Don't say my name. Don't think about me. Don't imagine how we can be together.

She walked through me, toward the living room. I buckled over in pain. It's always painful when you're standing in the way of the person you love, but I didn't care; I wanted to feel her so badly.

A moment later, I was flying to the liquor store. Disguised as an old, bearded homeless man, I put a bottle on the counter.

"Expensive Scotch, wouldn't you say? Where'd you get the money?" the clerk said.

I pulled my billfold from my back pocket. "None of your fucking business." I handed him a hundred dollar bill. "Keep the change, dickface."

I went back to Evey's and continued drinking on the steps until Joel and Keith, the two stupid apes, walked up and rang the buzzer.

Brooklyn answered, "We'll be down in thirty seconds."

Five minutes later, Evey and Brooklyn weren't down yet. The apes were exchanging stories about "banging chicks"— their words, not mine—and I was drinking. No... I was guzzling. Joel and Keith's angels were nearby. I could see them in the shadows. I wondered if I should make friends.

I stumbled over. Keith's angel was a female wearing a kilt-like skirt. I could tell she belonged to Keith because of her proximity to him. I'll get to that later—it's complicated.

"Nice skirt," I said.

"Fuck you," she said in her thick Scottish accent.

"All right then," I said, "Right here, out in the open? You've got easy access. I'm game."

"Take a hike, buddy. You're drunk," said Joel's angel.

"What's everyone's problem? Geez." I gave them both a dirty look.

"You don't remember me at all, ye bastart?" the Scotty bitch said.

I looked her up and down, shaking my head. "Why would I remember you?"

"Maybe cause we had a Tinder date last week and you showed up pissed, you fuckin' dunderweed. Pissed like ya are now."

"All right, all right, it's coming back to me."

All of us redirected our attention to the steps where Evey and Brooklyn came prancing out. The proximity thing is when you're with a group of angels, we are always naturally positioned nearest our souls. We can transport our own bodies (think teleportation) when we are within a one hundred yard radius of our souls, but once that barrier is broken, we have to fly the distance. Meaning, once your soul is out of range, you have to get back in range in order to move your energy from one space to another within an instant. When you get too far away, you have to go looking for them like any other person. The fact that we can hear their voices from several miles away helps, but if they're not talking, well then you're screwed. This is how a lot of people get kidnapped or killed. Their angels were out of range.

Evey got out of range once when she was fifteen. I had been bored to death, sitting outside her childhood home in Oakland when she snuck out the back door and climbed her neighbor's fence to meet her boyfriend a couple of blocks away. He was sixteen and had just gotten his driver's license. T.J., that little shit. I was frantic, searching for her. I found them about three miles away in a Burger King parking lot, making out in his dad's Buick.

There was nothing I could do to stop that relationship. It was innocent and pure, and T.J. was actually a good kid until Evey told him she wanted to wait until she was eighteen to have sex. *Good girl.* He broke up with her.

Then there was Byron, her real first everything. He was

nice—good parents, good grades. They had sex in his parents' garage when Evey was seventeen. I took off the moment they started kissing, but I got to hear every word of their conversation about protection. I almost stepped in front of a bus that night.

Mona had sat me down afterward and asked what was wrong with me. I told her I was worried about Evey's heart getting broken. Mona had said, "It's not your job to protect her heart, just her body and soul."

What's the difference when you love someone?

I was walking down the street, mindlessly following Brooklyn, Evey, and the two dumbshits along with the bitchy Scottish angel and the other one.

Evey said to Brooklyn, "Where are we going? I have to get up early for work."

"Tomorrow's Sunday, you don't have to work, and we're going to Oakland. Joel got tickets to the Chainsmokers. Like you'd miss that."

Evey beamed. "I was going to work on some sketches, but who cares? You're right! This will be awesome. Tracey can sketch her own stupid jeans."

I got a sinking feeling whenever I heard Evey talk about being irresponsible. I wanted to jump inside of Keith's body, make him do something really stupid, and end the whole double date right there.

The Scot was skipping down the middle of the street, humming some stupid old folk tune. I ran up next to her. "Listen, I need to ask you for a favor." She ignored me and took flight. I tried to catch up to her in the air, but I couldn't. I was drunk and dizzy. I hit the ground a little too hard and fell over. I could hear her laughing.

"What's your name?" I yelled.

She popped up beside me. "Greer's the name. What the fuck do ye want?"

"Will you let me borrow Keith for a minute?"

"Ye are crazy, aren't ye?"

We were following the group onto the BART subway to head to Oakland. It was crammed with people, so we sat on top of the train with a bunch of other angels as we zipped along through the tunnels.

I had to yell at her over the noise of the train. "Please! I won't hurt him. I just know Evey is going to make some terrible mistake tonight. I'm just looking out for her and him. She's reckless right now. Been going through a lot." I was sobering up, and Greer looked as though she was buying it.

I popped down into the subway car. Evey was laughing hysterically at something Keith had said. Keith's blond shaggy hair was sprouting out everywhere below his low red beanie, which matched his red T-shirt. His jeans were hanging off of his ass, revealing his plaid boxers. So unoriginal, really not Evey's type at all.

Greer was standing behind me. "What's in it for me?"

"Take the night off. I won't tell anyone."

She glanced over at Joel's angel, who shrugged, and then whispered something in her ear.

"You gonna watch Joel as well?" Greer asked.

"Fine," I told her. A moment later they were gone.

As I stared at Evey, Brooklyn, Joel, and Keith, it hit me that I was now responsible for all of them. *No more drinking tonight,* I chanted over and over in my head.

When we got to the Fox Theater, I saw Keith hand something to Brooklyn. She popped it into her mouth. The crowd was thick inside, and I was trying to stay as close to all of them as possible, hoping they wouldn't separate. Evey and Keith made it to the bar and did shots while Joel and Brooklyn watched the beginning of the show.

As a tipsy Evey made her way into the crowd, I decided I had had enough hovering for one night, so I popped into Keith's body.

I heaved audibly at his sick odor and weak body. Evey was the only human who smelled pleasant to me. I felt sluggish in his baby boy chest.

"What's wrong?" Evey's musical voice came at me. Her big brown eyes were wide and her smile timid.

"Nothing," I said. His voice was high, raspy, and super fucking annoying.

Evey and I, disguised as Keith, approached Brooklyn and Joel. Brooklyn immediately grabbed Evey and started dancing. She had Evey's hands up over her head and was running her fingers down the undersides of Evey's arms, and Evey was giggling.

She broke away from Brooklyn and came up to me and said, "I want one too!"

"One what? And why is Brooklyn acting so weird?"

Evey threw her arms over my (Keith's) shoulders and leaned into my ear. "Uh, duh, because she's rolling. Aren't you the one who gave her the X?"

I pulled back. "Me?" I put my hand over my chest.

She reached into my pocket and brushed my (Keith's) semi-hard dick in the process. "Oh." She smiled.

I wanted to throw up.

She popped a pill into her mouth. "Thanks."

Oh shit! Things were getting out of hand.

I had to know what she was feeling, so I reached into my pocket, took out a round pill with a smiley face on it, and popped it into my mouth as well.

Joel looked at me and laughed. "You never do that shit, dude." Brooklyn and Evey were dancing next to us. "You're gonna bang that chick on X, huh?"

"Uh, uh, yeah, man."

Winging it had so many meanings at the moment. I was in way over my head. The real Keith wouldn't remember any of this tomorrow. I scurried off to the bathroom and stared at Keith's ugly face in the mirror. I could still hear Evey blabbering to Brooklyn about how cute Keith was, and that started a violent session of dry heaving within me.

As I leaned over the sink about to purge my (Keith's) right lung, a guy holding a beer approached. "You okay, man?"

I almost swiped his beer. I needed a drink that badly, but I had to control myself. Instead, I turned toward the urinals, removed Keith's sad excuse for a dick, and peed. The size and shape of Keith's dick truly saddened me, not because Evey would appreciate it but because I couldn't understand how he was going to use it to do anything worthwhile. It was also really weird to hold onto another guy's dick. But I wasn't a guy; I was an angel. I had to constantly remind myself of that fact.

Heading back onto the theater floor, I found the girls and tried to collect myself.

After about an hour, the headlining act was on, playing the song "Roses." Evey was hanging all over me, smiling. I was trying to remain calm.

"I like you," she yelled over the music, then she mouthed

the lyrics, *Say you'll never let me go* as she swayed from side to side.

I felt my hands moving of their own accord, up her slim hips to her sides, then I was kissing her and cupping her breast—or rather, Keith was kissing her and cupping her breast. *Oh my God, what am I doing?*

Everything was vibrant. I was aware of the hair on Keith's arms standing up and his dick twitching every time Evey brushed against it. Her smell was stronger. Her breath, her sweat was intoxicating. I forgot all about booze for a couple hours and just let myself get lost in her. I blame the X.

What I was doing was wrong on so many levels. Doing ecstasy wasn't exactly a justification for a celestial being breaking every rule in the universe. Evey's tongue was in my mouth, and she grinding against me. God, it really seemed like she had it bad for this guy.

"I want to go home," she said, wiggling her eyebrows.

"Really?"

"I told you... I like you, Keith."

Maybe she sensed it was me. Maybe I wanted her to.

She kissed me again and then pulled back and stared into my eyes. I had to look away—I didn't want to remind her. Zack and Mona were right; I hadn't zapped her well enough. Brooklyn and Joel sucked face the entire taxi ride back. At least they were all safe. For the most part, I was sober and had held up my end of the deal with Abigail, Greer, and what's his face.

Joel and I followed the girls up to their apartment. I debated whether I should let good ol' limp-dick Keith have his body back. My decision was made once I followed Evey into her room. With one zip, she was literally standing in a thong and nothing else.

"Really?" I said derisively. "Really, Evelyn?"

She scowled then covered her breasts. "My full name? Honestly, what's up with the dad thing? I thought we were going to... I thought you liked me."

I had hurt her feelings. "No, don't cover up, you're just... you're just so fucking beautiful, so fucking bold." My eyes were wide.

She let her hands drop. What I wanted to say was, *Come on, Evey, seriously, this guy? You get naked like that for this guy?*

I hadn't seen her completely naked since she was a baby. I didn't know grown-up Evey's body at all. Yet ironically, I knew her better than I knew myself. My hands were drawn to her. We were in her room, alone, standing in the small space between her bed and the door. She walked toward me and pressed her body to mine—or rather, Keith's—reached her hands up around my neck, and smiled at me. She was searching my eyes again. It was freaking me out.

"There's something so familiar about you," she said.

I kissed her lightly and let my hands fall to her hips. I traced her thin waist with my fingertips as I moved my lips to her throat and collarbone. She moaned.

"Evelyn..." I sighed. I was tormented, tortured, conflicted, hungry for her but wanting to protect her.

She squinted. "That's funny that you call me Evelyn. Only my mother and grandmother call me that." She shrugged, leaned forward and tried to kiss me again.

I put my finger to her mouth. "I can't do this."

She stepped back, took a deep breath, and covered her body again, this time shamefully. She reached for a T-shirt lying on the bed and threw it on. "What is your deal? One minute you're all over me. I take my clothes off and you act repulsed, then you say I'm fucking beautiful and then say you can't do this?"

I walked toward her and put my hands on her shoulders to comfort her. Then I did something really despicable. "I'm impotent, Evey. I have very extreme erectile dysfunction. It's a medical condition and I take medication for it, but I can't mix it with the X. It could be a fatal."

Her eyes shot open with sympathy. "Oh, I'm so sorry. How embarrassing. I didn't know." It was almost like she adored Keith even more. My plan was backfiring. "You poor thing," she said as she wrapped her arms around my waist and hugged me.

I had to get her and Keith to sleep so I could get out of his ugly, dumb body. "You know what I would love, Evey? I would love to just lie down, call it a night. I'll take your number, and we'll go on a proper date."

Her eyes lit up. "I would love that too."

She put on a pair of flannel pajamas with penguins on them then patted the space on the bed next to her. "Come lie down. I'm so sorry, Keith. I hate that I put that pressure on you."

Geez, was she really into this guy?

"Don't apologize. I've been trying to sort it out for a long time." I was actually starting to feel kind of bad for Keith myself.

She cuddled up into the crook of my (Keith's) skinny arm, and it felt like heaven. I'd never actually been to heaven. I'm not even sure it exists. I know it's weird, an angel who's never been to heaven. No one had confirmed or denied that there was a place humans went when they died. But as I lay there with Evey, even in Keith's body, I started to think maybe heaven was on Earth. Maybe being an angel was like being in hell.

I waited until she dozed off, jumped out of Keith's body and sat in the corner to make sure he didn't react. He startled, looked around, and then down at Evey asleep, looking beautiful and serene. He smiled, closed his eyes. He was out. Thank God he didn't freak.

At magic hour, I passed Joel's angel, who said, "Hey, thanks, man, good job."

I'd actually done something right, sort of, but I was dying for a drink. I flew to the market where Henry, one of the banished angels, worked. I wanted to get myself a nice little bottle of Scotch. But instead of Henry, an irritated Mona was posing as the corner market cashier... that bitch!

"Really, you? Where's Henry?" I asked.

"Really yourself? I gave him the night off. I knew you'd be here. I know about that stunt you pulled earlier."

"I'm tired. I had a long day at work. I still did my job. In fact, I was on quadruple duty tonight, if you hadn't noticed. Some angels have no work ethic—like Abigail, for example. Why don't you get on her shit?" I shrugged, grabbed the bottle, and headed out the door.

Mona called after me, "She's not on probation. You are, Lucian." A moment later, Mona appeared at my side and put her hand on the bottle. She focused her beady little eyes on me. "All I'm saying is to take it easy on the booze. I know you're dealing with a lot right now."

I squinted at her. "You mean you're actually capable of feeling compassion? I need my paycheck please."

She scoffed and then pulled an envelope from her pocket and handed it to me. "Don't push me. Don't spend all this money on alcohol either. Go enjoy your hours. Get laid for God's sake, Lucian."

"For God's sake? Really, Mona? Why not for my sake?" I yelled. "Why is everything for him?"

She flew off in the other direction, mumbling something about being underpaid.

I drank only half the bottle on Evey's stoop before cutting myself off. Proud moment. I was really growing up after two thousand years. I popped into Evey's room because I hadn't heard any noise and I wanted to make sure everyone was still breathing. They were. It smelled like bad breath—Keith's, not hers of course.

They were fine, all wrapped up in each other. Magic hour was over, and time was speeding up, which was sometimes dizzying for angels. When I stumbled back against Evey's dresser, she startled awake. She shouldn't have been able to hear me. She jerked and inadvertently woke Keith up.

"Hey, babe," he said groggily.

What a dweeb.

"Babe?" Evey asked.

"Yeah, we had a crazy night last night, huh?"

"What are you talking about?" Oh no, this was all going to blow up in my face. She leaned in toward Keith's, to look into his eyes. "You look different. You seem different."

"I don't really remember much from last night," Keith said. "I think I blacked out. Did we do it?"

"No, remember, you said you were... that you had..." She glanced toward his pants area.

Keith jumped out of bed. "I don't know what you're

talking about. You don't have to be a bitch."

I was about to slap this fool, but then I realized it was kind of my fault. I moved across the room and knelt by Evey's bed. "Let him leave," I whispered. "Let him walk away."

She was staring off into space. Could she hear me?

"I was nice to you about it," she said weakly as Keith tied his shoes at the edge of the bed.

"I was fucked up. I don't remember anything."

"Okay, I get it," Evey said.

I was hurting her. Even though I was trying to protect her, doing everything I could to make sure she was safe, she was still getting her feelings hurt after having so much sweetness and compassion. She still looked to be zoning out.

"Let him go, Evey," I whispered again.

Keith left without saying good-bye. He slammed the door behind him.

"Fuck him," Evey said.

Thatta girl. She rolled over and fell asleep for the rest of the day.

That day went by in a rush. The sun sped past the horizon. It was night, and aside from Evey getting up to go to the kitchen for water and a short conversation with Brooklyn about how neither one of them had had sex, that was it for the day. Zack was on his phone outside, doing his bookie shit, and I was trying not to drink.

Then I realized that it was going to be a very long and boring night. I flew to the liquor store and got a bottle, came back, and sat next to Abigail on the stoop. Zack was sitting on her other side.

He said to her, "Why won't you go out with me?"

She ignored him. I pounded the whiskey and stared off into space.

Ten minutes later, he asked again. "Just one date?"

She ignored him again.

I had had enough of her. "Abigail, you snooty bitch, will you please fucking answer him?"

"Fuck you, Lucian." She flew off before I could respond.

"Nice one," Zack said.

A moment later, he was gone too. I was alone. I finished the bottle and went into Evey's room.

Bad idea. She was reading in bed. I knelt next to her. She set the book on the nightstand and looked at the ceiling.

"Hello?" she said.

"Hi," I whispered, knowing she couldn't hear me or see me.

She squinted. Could she hear me?

"Hi," I said again.

She squeezed her eyes shut and shook her head. How could she hear me? Was I messing with her? What was happening?

I bent near her ear and whispered, "Evey, next time, in the next life we'll be together—that's how this will be corrected. This will be righted. This can't be our forever fate. Next time we'll live together, we'll die together. We'll experience every war together, inside ourselves and outside in the world. We won't be out of reach, unavailable, unattainable, just love longing to be. Let's keep moving fast in opposite directions. Keep praying we meet on the other side. I'll see you there; I know I will. I have to believe that. Watch for me. I'll be barreling toward you, arms wide open, and then we'll crash into each other with the force of two spent lives yearning to be one."

When her eyes opened, one stray tear trickled down her cheek. I touched her shoulder, and she relaxed. She squeezed her eyes shut again, took three deep breaths, then dozed off. I wished I could hear her thoughts.

I took Mona's advice and got on Tinder. It really was a disgusting mechanism, but I was horny. During magic hour that night, I met Zina in room 1203 at the St. Francis Hotel. We had a corner room with frilly old-timey curtains and a floral bedspread.

"This is the old part of the building," Zina said as she kicked off her heels.

She was tall with very dark hair and wings. Yeah, the carpet always matched the drapes. Blond angels had blond wings and so on. She was exotic and similar to me, which meant we were both old. Think operating systems on your iMac. We were basically the same version. As time went on, with each new version, God or someone got lazy. The older angels were stronger and better-looking, in my opinion. By the way, I've heard Jobs is one of us now, so don't expect Apple to crash and burn anytime soon.

"You're about my age, huh?"

She was undressing with no modesty. "No, I'm older. We've met. You don't remember me?"

"I drink a lot."

She sat on the bed in her expensive lingerie and crossed her legs. She was trying to recall when we had met before. "I think it was the late fourteen hundreds."

"Da Vinci," we said at the same time.

"I remember now," I said. Somehow, even after my little debacle with Joanie "I speak to God" Arc, Mona had still been willing to assign me to da Vinci. Those were prideful years for me.

"I'm still kind of pissed at him for making me ugly in the *Vitruvian Man*. And my you-know-what was not exactly to scale. He didn't want other, less fortunate men to get a complex."

"Mmkay," Zina said. "So you revealed yourself to him."

I undressed and sat down next to her. "We were great friends. I trusted him. We trusted each other."

"Is it true that he was...?"

"What? Gay? I don't know. If I knew, I wouldn't tell you anyway. He was the most interesting man I've ever met. Truly a genius and a workhorse. He was tireless. I only revealed myself to help him more. The Plate tectonics theory was all me." I grinned.

Zina had a fluttering, cautious laugh like a wise, classy woman. My dick twitched.

"It's coming back to me," I said. "You were playing a courtesan in Venice. A poet. I thought you were a human at first. I didn't understand what that was all about. How you were able to hide your wings from me."

"Old trick of the trade. I'll teach you. Anyway, those years were a mistake. I was trying to protect one of my souls at the time—a young woman who was selling herself cheaply and dangerously. I was teaching her the ropes, or trying to."

"So you revealed yourself?"

"That was the only time, and I regret it. She fell madly in love with me, and I with her. She took her own life after I tried to remove myself from her thoughts. Something went terribly wrong." Zina looked as though she was about to cry. She shook the thoughts away. "That was a long time ago."

Zina was definitely older than me but not by much. I could tell by the way she talked. After hearing Zina's story, I felt sick over what I had done to Evey. I worried about her.

"You and I slept together, didn't we?"

She laughed again. "Am I that forgettable?"

"No," I said instantly. "You're gorgeous... captivating."

A moment later, our bodies were connected. I moved in and out of Zina, caressing her smooth skin while she made beautiful sounds. Her wings were spread high above her head, and her hands were bracing my sides. We moved together for a long time. It felt good, but something was missing. I finally came twenty minutes later when I closed my eyes and thought about Evey.

Zina and I respectfully washed each other in the shower.

She stood on her tippy toes and kissed my forehead. "You're different than the others, Lucian."

"I know."

She smiled. "You're hopeless."

"I know," I said, my voice barely audible.

Magic hour was ending, and I wanted to get back to Evey. When I hit the street, everything was moving fast. I was so dizzy I almost fell down.

"Shit," I said, looking at my watch, which was frozen. It had stopped working.

"What's wrong?" Zina said, standing beside me.

"How much time has passed since the magic hours ended?"

She checked her phone. "About forty-five minutes. I'm sure your souls will be fine. It's early."

"Soul," I said mindlessly. "I gotta run." I kissed her cheek and took flight.

7

OBLIVION

Evelyn

MY DREAMS HAVE always been nonsensical—until last night. I didn't know I was dreaming. I kept thinking I was exactly where I should be. I was with a man, familiar but mysterious. He was sexy and cocky, and he was feeding me. We were on a date at a restaurant, laughing and having smart conversation. A minute later, he changed. His expression dropped, he squinted, and at once, he seemed lovesick and tormented. He was whispering to me, but I couldn't hear what he was saying. I closed my eyes to try to listen closely, and when I opened them, we were standing side by side, still and naked like winter trees in a creek. There was nothing around us but darkness. When I shivered, he touched my hand and I was warm.

"Who are you?" I asked him.

"Lucian."

I could hear his voice. It was rough, pained. That was the end.

When I woke up from the dream, I started crying because I remembered him. I knew him and I didn't know how. I knew his scent, his voice, his angled features, his full lips, and his searching eyes. I knew his warmth, his touch, and the comfort I felt near him. But awake, I was longing for him. It was excruciating. I was losing my mind. I was being fanatical, paranoid, melodramatic. None of those things were typical of me. I had always been pragmatic and certain of what was and what wasn't out there.

I went to the kitchen in my sweats and grabbed my keys. Brooklyn was sitting at the round table, slurping up cereal.

"You're up early," she said.

"I'm leaving. Going to Tracey's house to work on the denim. I'm really behind and need to catch up on some things. I have to get going."

"You look like shit, Pinky."

"Hey, Brooklyn, I hate that nickname. I've always wanted to tell you that."

"I thought you liked it," she whined.

"I got pink eye from your house two days before our prom. I'm a little bitter about it."

"Sheesh, I thought we were cycle sisters. You shouldn't have PMS for another two weeks. Or are you just being emo cause you didn't get laid the other night?"

I rolled my eyes and shook my head. She was impossible. "Brooklyn, do we know someone named Lucian? Like a really good-looking guy, wears black, maybe longish hair, a touch of facial scruff."

Through a mouthful of Cocoa Puffs, she mumbled, "No, sounds hot though."

"Wings," I said.

"I'm sorry, what?"

"He might have wings."

She spit out her cereal. "Wings?"

I nodded. "Wings."

"Aww, honey, have you been eating? You do look emaciated. Or are you hallucinating from the X still? Geez, did Keith slip you something else? Should I drive you to work?"

"No." I shook my head. Brooklyn was a terrible driver, but anyway, I wanted to be alone. "I'm fine, just had a weird dream."

"I'd say."

"I'll be at Tracey's in San Rafael. I hate that I have to drive all the way out there when we should be working in the warehouse. She's such a lazy bitch." I was trying to change the subject.

"You mentioned something to me about angels a couple days ago. What's going on, Evey? You want to find a church and go pray or something?"

Brooklyn had been raised atheist. She had a total, absolute disconnect from anything religious or spiritual besides her mom's religion of vegetarianism.

"No, no, I'm fine. Gonna head to work."

I drove fast and recklessly. I missed him. Why? Him—who was him?

"Lucian!" I yelled as I drove fast across the Golden Gate Bridge. "Lucian!"

When I got to the other side of the bridge, I pulled into a space in the Vista Point parking lot and shut off my engine. I called my mom.

"Hi, honey," she answered.

I hadn't seen or talked to my mom in three weeks since I had told her I hated her for being so hard on me. My words were harsh toward the woman who had brought me into this world, but I had had years of resentment built up toward her. I had always been closer to my dad because I could do no wrong in his eyes. But my mom despised Brooklyn and thought fashion was silly and would never look at my sketches. It hurt me. It drove a wedge between us. I wanted her approval more than anyone's, but she and I were different, and what I did didn't interest her. It was hard to accept that my own mother could be so selfish that she wouldn't even humor me by acting interested in what I had created. There were no siblings to talk it over with. I just had to learn to accept it. I couldn't change her, but I vowed if I ever had kids, I would never dismiss their passion by telling them that it was a pipe dream, or by saying it didn't interest me.

My parents were working-class Oakland lifers. My mom was a schoolteacher, and my dad was a UPS driver. They had been married for thirty-five years. The first ten they had spent trying to have a baby, then I came along. And I'm the only one. Imagine the pressure.

"Mom, I'm sorry about what I said to you at dinner." I was going to take the high road.

"It's been three weeks."

"I know," I said.

"I was giving you space, but I didn't think it would take

you this long. Better late than never, I guess. I appreciate the apology, Evelyn. I only want the best for you."

"Mom, what is your idea of 'the best for me'?"

"Some stability, that's all." *Here we go again.*

"I'm twenty-five. Stability is right up there with doing my taxes."

She laughed. "You're so spirited."

Something came over me. "Speaking of—how come we never went to church?"

"Where are you right now, Evelyn? Shouldn't you be at work?"

I got out of my car and walked toward the lookout. "I'm looking at the Golden Gate. I'm headed to Tracey's. I just pulled over because I was thinking about you and I wanted to call you." It was true. I had been thinking about her and the mysterious Lucian.

"We didn't go to church because your grandparents were extremely staunch, devout Catholics who beat each other in front of me, told lies, were hypocrites, cheated on each other, and then divorced. It kind of left a bad taste in my mouth."

My mom's candor was shocking. "I can't believe you just said all of that."

"I don't want you to hate me, Evey. I'm human; I make mistakes. I won't always get it right, but I love you more than anything in this world, more than myself, and I want so badly for you to be happy. Your father and I didn't take you to church, but we tried to be an example of love and honesty. We tried to show you that life can be fulfilling, that couples can be happy, and that you can be happy and have pride in what you do. But we also don't want to see you fail. We don't want to see you heartbroken either."

"I have to decide what makes *me* happy. And maybe you have to let me fail sometimes, Mom. Maybe I need to experience a broken heart for once. You can't control everything."

"I know. I'm sorry I've been pressuring you." A few seconds of silence passed before she added, "You have so much spirit. You're someone's muse—probably someone up there. You don't have to go to church to believe in a higher power, sweetie. That's all I'm saying."

"Thanks, Mom."

"You want to talk to your dad? He took the day off. He's here."

"Sure."

She handed him the phone.

"Hi, DD." My dad had always called me DD La Rue. DD for Darling Daughter. Even my mom had started calling me that sometimes.

"Hi, Dad. How are you?"

"Good. Your mom is making me banana macadamia nut pancakes. I can't complain."

"I miss you."

"Miss you too, DD. Come see us, we're not that far. I saw that you were at that concert in Oakland. Two miles from the house."

It stung that I had hurt him. "How'd you know?"

"Facebook, silly."

"Ha! Well, I was on a date."

"Anything serious? A good guy?" he asked.

"I thought I liked him, but in the end, he wasn't who I thought he was. I'm sure I won't see him again. No big deal."

"Be safe, my Darling Daughter."

"Always, Dad."

We said I love yous and good-byes, and then hung up. I headed toward the pedestrian path on the bridge. I needed ten extra minutes before dealing with Tracey. It was a crisp and clear morning. No San Francisco fog in sight. I shivered from the breeze as I walked quickly toward the center of the bridge. I was chanting the name Lucian in my mind.

When I got to the middle, I leaned over and looked down. It was so far to the water that it was hard to see the detail in the rippling current. It was just a terrifying black void full of unknowns.

"Lucian, who are you?" I asked aloud.

I squinted, trying to see the movement of the water. The soft lapping against the beams of the bridge were actually waves beating violently against the concrete and steel. I leaned farther and farther until a gust of wind blew me back.

I could feel him. He was there.

8

CHOICES

Lucian

"OH CHRIST, OH God, what is she doing?" I was barreling toward her so fast I could feel my wings cramping.

She had said my name. I had been lost, tormented, looking everywhere for her. I'd gone to the apartment, but she was gone. Abigail had no idea where Evey was. She mumbled something about Evey leaving really early to go do denim for Tracey. Abigail wouldn't even look up from her phone to talk to me. I wanted to slap her for not caring. Cursing loudly, I flew to the warehouse, but it was empty. I headed toward the bridge, and that was when I heard Evey say my name.

I was flying toward her. She was leaning over the guardrail almost entirely, her feet dangling off the ground. I pushed the air toward her. She gasped and found her footing back on the walkway. I sat perched on the railing, poised and ready to react. I wondered what she was doing. She squinted, staring straight forward, then she jumped up and dangled over the railing again, farther this time. I popped into a body walking by and appeared behind her. It was a male, attractive, around her age.

"Hey there, what are you doing? That looks dangerous," I said to her.

Her body stiffened, and her feet hit the ground. She waited five whole seconds before turning around and looking at me. Taking a step closer, she stared into my eyes. Her mouth was slack, as if she couldn't find her voice.

"Do you want me to call someone for you?" I asked.

She stepped even closer. She was studying me with intense focus. "I know it's you," she said quietly, barely loud enough for a normal person to hear over the wind and traffic.

"Excuse me?" I said.

"I know you're in there, Lucian."

I blinked. *Fuck.* "Sweetie, I think I should call someone for you."

"I can smell you. I can tell it's you."

I hadn't zapped her good enough. It occurred to me that I could zap her again in that moment, but I didn't. She reached for my hand, but I pulled it back. I was going to try to convince her.

"What is your name?"

"You know my name," she shot back. "I remember. It's like a foggy dream. We held each other, but I remember. You were in my house, in my bed. I know it's true."

It was hard to continue lying to her. "Do you have a car in

the parking lot that I can walk you to?"

"If you don't know me at all, why don't you leave me alone?"

"I'm concerned for you. You seem troubled. And you're basically hanging off this enormous bridge. It's dangerous."

"Leave me alone," she said.

I needed to try a different approach. I smiled, fairly certain this guy had a nice enough face. She didn't smile back. "It's not every day you see a gorgeous woman dangling precariously over the rail of the Golden Gate."

"I'm no damsel in distress."

"No?" I couldn't take my eyes off of her mouth.

She came closer. *What is she doing?* She leaned forward.

"Kiss me, Lucian," she whispered near my ear. "I want you to kiss me, but I want it to be Lucian."

I couldn't control it. I couldn't stop myself. I couldn't deny her.

When I left the stranger's body and revealed myself to her, our mouths collided. We were kissing, our tongues twisting, our hands going everywhere. I spread my wings as far and wide as I could to wrap them around us as we kissed. We were cloaked, invisible to the rest of the world. Only Evey could see that we were cocooned by a curtain of black feathers.

She pulled away from my mouth, breathless. She was putty in my arms.

"I want you," she said. "I want you inside of me."

Zack's voice echoed in my mind. *The only way you can be together is to take her out.*

"Did you hear me? I want to be with you," she said before kissing me again.

I pulled away. "Like have sex?"

"Yes. That, and I want to be with you forever. I don't know how I know that. I just do. I'm in love with you, aren't I? And you did something to me?"

"It's a mind trick, Evey. You're meant to feel that way toward me." We were still huddled inside my wings.

"If we can't be together, I'll jump and you won't be able to stop me. I can feel in your fingertips how much you love me."

I touched her cheek and ran my fingertips down her jawline. It was true. Every cell in my body ached for her.

"Ahh, touch me everywhere, Lucian, please."

I kissed her hard. Her legs gave out. I held her body to mine. "Do you trust me?" I asked.

"More than anyone."

It pained me to hear that, knowing what I was about to do.

I flew up off the bridge, still holding Evey. She nestled into my chest like a sleeping baby, and I pressed my mouth to hers. She opened her eyes as we began falling fast toward the water. There was no fear in her body... yet. We kissed as we plummeted under the surface of the rigid bay water. Down and down we went, still kissing. I knew she wasn't breathing. I wasn't breathing either, but I could hold my breath for fifteen minutes—long enough to end Evey's life as a human.

After a minute, I started to feel her fear. She pulled away; her eyes were open and pleading. I held her tightly to my body. She began to gasp. She held onto my neck as she breathed in water. Her body began to jerk. She put her mouth on mine, seeking comfort. When she started convulsing, I gave up. That was it. I couldn't do it. I braced her against me and shot straight out of the water. I blew breaths into her mouth until she coughed. I was flying to her apartment as fast as I could.

Evey was out of it, trembling and gasping for air. "Why?" she tried to say as she coughed uncontrollably.

I got her into the apartment unnoticed. I carried her to the bathroom and started a warm bath. Her teeth were chattering as she tried to speak again. "Why?"

Standing her on her weak legs, I stripped her clothes from her shaking, blue body. "I'm so sorry," I said. My voice sounded like a cry. I picked up her naked body and placed her in the tub. She had the utmost trust for me still. I couldn't understand it.

Rubbing her arms and legs to warm her up, I chanted over and over, "I'm so sorry. Please forgive me. Take me, God, I can't bear this."

As if it weren't enough that I had almost killed the only living being that had ever meant anything to me, I was also feeling the intense effects of alcohol withdrawal. I was almost convulsing myself, and I was tortured by what I had done. All I could do was stare hopelessly into Evey's trusting, chocolaty eyes, so warm and so innocent. What had I done?

"Take me, God," I said again.

"Stop saying that, Lucian, please. I'm okay. I just don't understand anything. Are you shaking because you're cold? You can come in here with me."

I shook my head. "I'll tell you everything, but not right now. Right now we need to warm you up. I should not have done that. It was a mistake. I'm sorry. I promise I won't keep anything from you ever again." I owed it to her to tell her as much as I knew, and I planned to do just that.

After dressing her and carrying her to bed, I lay down beside her and stroked her hair. Her eyes were closed, but she was awake. She curled into my body, so I held her closer. I tightened my grip. I would never let her go.

"I feel like I'm on drugs when I'm with you," she said near my ear.

In a low voice, I told her, "I am so in love with you, Evey, but I can't be with you. I'm not allowed. You're in love with me because I am made to make you feel that way. I was never supposed to let you see me. Another angel told me that if I took your life, you would become like me and that we could be together."

"Do it," she said quietly.

She's going crazy. I caused this. "I told you why you feel that way. Please don't be reckless. I could never go through with it. It hurts so badly to say this, but we can never be together. I have to protect you. Don't you see that? I tried today, and it was the worst feeling I've ever had. I don't see how it would be possible."

"So what are you saying? That you'll try to make me forget you again? That I'll go on with the rest of my life with you hanging around while I have dreams of you... while I ache for you?" She remembered everything. I didn't know how I could make her forget. I was in unchartered territory.

"I ache for you. I've ached for you for so long. Since you've grown up, I've wanted to be with you. When you were young, I wanted to teach you everything about the world. I wanted to protect you. I still do, and this is the only way I can. I have to follow the rules so that I can be here for you forever."

She laced her fingers between mine. "You're warm. Why

are you trembling?"

"I'm an alcoholic," I told her.

Her eyes opened wide. "You are?"

I nodded.

"You're so human," she said, "so flawed. I love you more because of it."

"I know it feels that way, but I'm not human. Flawed, yes, but not human."

"I can help you get sober, if that's what you want. We can be together. What's going to happen if we're together?" she asked.

I knew she could. Not being able to have her was half of the reason I drank, or maybe it was the whole reason I drank. "I don't know what will happen, but I'm too scared to find out. I don't want to risk your life anymore."

"I'll never get over you," she said.

We kissed again.

She removed my T-shirt and ran her hand down the muscles of my back. "They're gone. You're so human."

She took off her own clothes, and I didn't stop her. I just looked on in awe. Why hadn't Mona shown up? Why hadn't someone intervened?

We were naked, and I took her in, running my hands up her smooth sides, cupping her breasts, teasing her. Things sped up, and we were kissing frantically. I put my hand between her legs and touched her.

"Ahh, Lucian. Make love to me."

"I'm going to, but let's slow down." I was still waiting for someone to come and remove me from the situation.

Just let me have this one night, God, Mona, whoever.

I kissed my way down her body, sucking her nipple into

my mouth while my hand teased her below. She reached down and touched me, taking me in her hand, stroking me.

"Please, I want you," she pleaded.

God, it felt so good. There was no way I could stop. I had never made love to a human. I didn't know what would happen. As I kissed farther down, she writhed beneath my touch. We knew how to move with each other.

"I love touching you. I love that you can feel me," I told her.

I still couldn't believe she wanted me to take her life so we could be together. The shakes had stopped. I was calm, content, in heaven. I felt as though I was on drugs too as I kissed her smooth skin. Then my mouth was on her, between her legs, sucking and teasing. Her body was perfect, and the sounds she made were beautiful. I couldn't stop.

Her hands were in my hair, and she was pressing her body to my mouth. I had never tasted anything so sweet. I would quit the bottle to have that every day. She pulled me up to kiss her mouth.

"You taste so good," I said.

She shivered. I was holding myself over her, looking into her eyes.

"I love you," she said.

"I love you too."

She spread her legs wide. "I need you now, Lucian."

A moment later, I was inside her. We were one, moving with ease and grace, kissing and touching and gripping. I had never felt anything so good in my long, long life. Her heat was so arousing, I thought I was going to lose it. I moved up on my knees, still connected. I touched and teased her while I stayed moving inside of her. She arched her back. The sounds stopped; I felt her tightening around me. I let my body fall forward so that our mouths could connect again. She wasn't breathing—she was coming, and so was I.

It was surreal. She was just reduced to nothing. She whimpered and then held my head to her chest.

"Jesus," she breathed.

"Lucian," I corrected.

She laughed then, and I laughed too. All of the weight of the universe, the unknown, the rules, God, and what would become of the two of us just dissipated. It vanished and we became two people giving and taking from each other all in the same.

We spent the entire day in bed, goofing off, making love, and getting to know Lucian and Evey in a completely new way. That was the moment when I started to change my mind and believe that we could actually be together.

9

LOVE
Evelyn

"WELL, WE HAVEN'T turned into pumpkins yet," I said, curling my naked self into Lucian's strong body. It was the afternoon... we were still in bed.

His chest rumbled as he said, "'We haven't yet,' is right. You can't tell anyone, Evey. Who knows what will happen?"

"I figured that. Anyway, who would believe me? But are you going to stay here, with me?" He knew I wanted him to. I didn't have to say it.

He seemed more resolute than before. "Yes. I'll have to meet with Mona later. You'll be sleeping. I need to talk to her. I'll find out if there's anything we can do."

"How are you doing, having not had a drink?"

"I'm fine. I haven't even thought about it. I really only

developed that habit in the last couple of years." He squinted, searching my eyes as if he was trying to read my mind. "Is it strange for you, knowing that I've watched you grow up?"

"No." I had thought about it earlier but decided it wasn't strange at all. "It's not. It's oddly comforting." I had a lot of questions for him, but I was content to stay in bed with him forever and pretend like everything was completely normal.

"Evelyn, do you have questions for me? Do you want to know things about us? About you and me? I had to..."

"It's a little fuzzy, like when we met in the bar and when you told me who you were."

"Yeah. I didn't want to do it, but I had to..." He swallowed. He was hesitating and nervous. I felt his heart speed up.

"Did you do something to me?"

"I had to make you forget me," he said. "I'm sorry."

"Just tell me what you did."

"We use our thumbs and press them to your—"

"I remember."

"You do? You remember a lot, don't you?"

"You told me you loved me." I sat up. "I remember, you said, 'I'll always be here for you.'"

"I don't know how it's possible, but it didn't work on you. It was temporary."

"How many times have you done that to me?"

"That was the only time, I swear to you, Evey."

"Swear to God?" I demanded.

He smirked. "Really?"

"Yes, really."

"I swear to God. It was the one and only time I have ever tried to erase your memory. I'm good at what I do. I normally wouldn't have to do that. But swearing to God..."

"What? It's frowned upon?"

"No, it's just meaningless. People shouldn't lie to each other to begin with. People shouldn't have to fear hell in order to tell the truth. They should fear that their lies will ruin relationships or get them in trouble, here now, on Earth, with the people they love."

"You sound human when you say that, Lucian."

"It's what I've always wanted for you... real truth. I can't tell you what will happen once you're gone from this Earth. How is that for faith? I can tell you for sure though that there are consequences to your actions here, while you're living."

"You were Keith the other night, weren't you?"

He nodded, and then rolled onto his back and stared up at the ceiling. I thought he was avoiding making eye contact with me. I wondered if he had felt guilty for the stunt he pulled in Keith's body.

"*You* were actually Keith?" I asked again.

He nodded again. I started laughing hysterically. Lucian was trying to control his own laughter.

"So the erectile dysfunction thing was your way of keeping me off him?"

"Yes." He chuckled. "I'm not proud. Lies, Evey, all lies. I regret getting myself into that mess."

I stopped laughing. "Why didn't you just make love to me as Keith? I was obviously willing."

"Yeah, you were all over him." He seemed irritated by that fact.

"Why didn't you let him make love to me?"

"It wouldn't have been love for you, not with him. And if I had gotten out of his body and let you guys... you know? It wouldn't have been love for him either. I had overheard him earlier. He wasn't into making love that night. He just wanted to have sex with you. I'm sorry, Evey. I hate telling you that. I was trying to protect you."

"So he wasn't into me?"

"He was into you. You're beautiful. No man on this planet wouldn't be into you, but that night Keith wanted to party. It would not have been special for you or for him. Trust me."

"Maybe I didn't need special." He grimaced. "Anyway, I sensed that it was you, once we were in the club," I said. "You could have made love to me as Keith."

I was lying in bed, naked, next to this celestial creature, and he was just a man to me. A beautiful, jealous, kind, loving, possessive man.

"I wouldn't have been able to satisfy you as Keith." He smirked. "Let's just leave it at that."

Then we were kissing again.

Of course I had a lot of questions. Questions like, "Am I dreaming? Is this possible?" I'd had a hard time believing in the tooth fairy as a child, let alone the fact that someone or something had been following me around my entire life and that that something or someone looked like this guy. When I was a teenager, I had actually thought that the government was a sham, so religion was total fiction to me. That's how cynical I was. I had thought love was a choice not a feeling. Of course that could have been due to Brooklyn's negative influence after we had become old enough to date. Somehow, every guy, regardless of how much I liked him, eventually turned into a buffoon by the end of the night. I wondered though if maybe Lucian had more to do with that than Brooke.

"So why Beckett? He was a good guy," I said.

"Evey, Beckett is the worst kind. I know messing with him the way that I did was not right. I blame the whiskey, but I'm glad I did. Beckett is not what you think. He had a date lined up after you. He was texting her in the bathroom."

"You're kidding me?"

"No." He frowned. "I hate telling you stuff like that. There's no reason for it. It has nothing to do with you."

"It seemed like he liked me."

"He did. He liked you, and he liked some girl named Karla and another girl named Michelle. It's just his age. He gets a lot of attention, and he likes it. He'll always be that way though. I've been around for a long time. Men like that don't commit because they need a lot of attention, all the time. He's like Brooklyn's male counterpart."

"Well, that makes sense." And it did, once I thought of Beckett in those terms. "Maybe we should set him and Brooklyn up."

"No, they'd fight over who had more prospects." He laughed.

"True. But I don't believe that Brooklyn will be single forever. I think her whole MO is just a front."

"Maybe. I don't think she's a horrible person or friend, Evey. I just think she's taken you for granted."

"How do you feel about me?"

He rolled onto his side to face me while brushing the hair out of my face. I studied his angled jaw, his black hair, his piercing eyes. "Evelyn, I've existed for more than two millennia. In two thousand years, I have watched over so many lives. At times, more than five souls were my responsibility alone. I've watched all of them die. I've held many of them while they were dying. It's in my nature to do that, to give peace to my souls, to look out for them when I can, to sway the good ones to do the right thing, and to protect man and life here on Earth. I've watched over stunningly beautiful and brilliant women, but I have never felt love for any human the way I feel it for you. You are literally the air in my lungs."

I was breathless for a moment. "You don't have to say that."

"It's true. I want you to understand the difference, the magnitude. When you started dating, I went crazy. I was drinking every day, all day, worried that some asshole was going to break your heart, and at the same time, I was jealous that I couldn't be with you, that I couldn't be the one you laughed with, the one you made love to, the one you shared your life with."

"Lucian..."

"Listen"—he put his hand on my cheek—"I can't bear being without you. I don't know what you've done to me, but I'm willing to risk it all, my life ten times over, to be near you. Watching you with other men was torture. I couldn't take it, Evey, so I made the decision to reveal myself to you. I wanted to get banished or be resigned. I never expected that I would get to be with you this way. I feel alive now. I regret nothing."

I wanted to reciprocate. To tell him the pull toward him was so strong it haunted my dreams, but he already knew that. I didn't have to say anything. I kissed him gently, tugging at his beautiful bottom lip. When he closed his eyes, I said, "So you meant to show me who you really are? It wasn't an accident and you knew there would be some consequence?"

"Love is selfish, isn't it?"

We both flinched at the sound of Brooklyn fixing something in the kitchen.

"What do I tell her? She's going to wonder why I'm not at work. She's going to wonder about you. Are you just going to disappear? Is that the way it will be? You pop in and out whenever you want, and I never know where you are?"

"No, I promise I won't do that to you. Tell her you met me a few weeks ago. Tell her I'm your boyfriend." He smiled—boyish, sweet, innocent... human.

I sat up on the edge of the bed. "Do you want some coffee or something?"

"Yeah, I'd love some." He caressed my naked back. "You are so fucking beautiful it hurts."

When he sat up behind me, I felt his body expand. I closed my eyes and heard the sound of his wings spreading. Suddenly they were around me, and I felt as though my body and mind had drifted off somewhere into space... into heaven.

"Does that feel good?"

I could barely speak. He was sucking and kissing my neck, gripping my hair with one hand and teasing my breast with the other.

"Lucian," I whispered, "I will never get anything done if you don't stop touching me." What I wanted to say was that he was ruining me for all others, that nothing would compare to the way he made me feel.

"I can't help it," he said.

He removed his hands. I opened my eyes and his wings were gone and he was just a man, albeit a ridiculously gorgeous man. He had the sheet over his lap, and he was smirking with confidence. He knew he had gotten me all hot and bothered. He was a god, truly, a perfect specimen.

"No one will believe you want to be with me," I told him.

"Stop being insecure. You have no reason to be. You're insanely gorgeous. Even during your awkward stage, you were beautiful."

When I scowled, he laughed. "Awkward stage?" I crossed my arms and pouted.

"Yeah, like between eleven and fourteen, the acne... yowza!"

I socked him in his solid arm. "Ha ha, very funny. I'm going to make coffee even though it's three in the afternoon."

I put on a T-shirt and underwear. My hair was going in every direction, and I could feel the permanent flush on my face. When I walked into the kitchen Brooklyn was leaning against the counter, cutting tomatoes. She set the knife down without a word, and watched me go to the coffee pot to begin filling it.

"Have you been here the whole time? I thought you left this morning."

I was smiling and couldn't stop. "I did. I came back."

"When she ran into me at the café," came Lucian's voice.

We both turned around to take him in, standing in the doorway wearing nothing but a pair of black jeans sans boxers. *Dear God.*

Brooklyn's mouth was on the floor. She was taking ogling to a new level.

"Brooke," I said, "do you mind?"

"Hi," she said.

He approached her. "I'm Lucian."

"Lucian," she whispered, breathlessly.

"Yep," he said with a cocky grin. *Oh geez, he is full of himself when he's not drunk and emo.* He stretched out his arms, and Brooke and I fixated on his flexing muscles. "God, I feel great." He looked up at the ceiling and said, "I mean it, old man."

That was the first I had heard Lucian address God directly, and he had done it openly and humorously. I giggled. Brooklyn was still speechless.

"How do you two know each other?" she said finally.

"We go way back," Lucian replied.

"Well, not really," I corrected him. "He was in fashion school for a year before he dropped out."

He looked at me with a scowl and mouthed, "Really?"

"You never mentioned him... or wait, was this the thing you were rambling about this morning?" Brooklyn said. "What was the deal with the wings?"

"I was kidding." Brooklyn would buy anything. "I was feeling you out to make sure you hadn't bagged him and didn't want to tell me. He and I had lost touch, then I ran into him a few weeks ago, and we went on a couple dates."

She turned her back to Lucian and frowned at me before whispering, "Did you hide him from me because you were afraid he'd like me more?" That was how Brooklyn's mind worked. She could be arrogant and insulting in one sentence.

I didn't know if Lucian had heard her, but he crossed the kitchen in two large strides and kissed me. When my knees buckled, his hand went to the small of my back to hold me up.

"I missed you in there," he said. "Come back to bed."

"Jesus Christ," Brooklyn said in a rush of air.

Lucian turned to face her. "Something the matter, Brooklyn?"

He picked me up in one fell swoop and carried me back to my room. The whole time Brooklyn was looking on in shock.

Inside my room, I fake-whined, "But I never got my coffee."

He set me on the bed, left the room, and returned two minutes later with two cups of coffee. "She was still frozen in shock when I went into the kitchen, and then she tried to flirt with me. I really cannot believe you've put up with her crap all these years."

"She's not that bad," I said.

He shrugged and then sat down against the headboard and crossed his legs at the ankles. I couldn't stop staring at him.

"What, Evey?" His deep dimple appeared. It was cocky Lucian.

I gave in to him. "Nothing. You've had years to stare at me; I just want to look at you."

"That's fair." He winked.

I sat next to him and felt something sticking out of the sheet under my leg. It was a thick black feather. I held it up. "Looks like you lost one."

Lucian stared at it impassively. Several long, silent, strange seconds went by.

"What's wrong?" I said.

"That's impossible." He stood quickly, and his astounding wings were suddenly spread on full display. He was inspecting them.

After taking the feather from my hand, he pressed it to

his wing and let go, but it just drifted, slowly and sadly, to the floor as we both followed it with our eyes. Lucian's expression was pure horror. I was just confused.

"What? That doesn't happen?" I reached for it.

"Never," he said, staring off into space.

I held the feather for a second before it turned to ash.

"Poof," Lucian said, in shock.

"What does this mean?"

"I don't know."

He retracted his wings and plopped onto the bed. The first ungraceful thing I had ever seen him do. He sank down and curled into me, clearly seeking comfort.

"Are you okay?" I said.

"I don't know. I'll have to go see Mona tonight. She'll know." He closed his eyes.

I knew he didn't sleep, so I just held him. It was hard to believe I wasn't in panic mode. My whole world had shifted on its axis. Questions were running through my mind at hyper speed. For a moment, I thought everything I'd ever wanted to know could be answered. I could ask Lucian anything. The meaning of life was within my grasp, but strangely, this cocky, brilliant, funny, attractive celestial being was just a lost little boy who had been existing on sheer faith like so many of us. He knew little more than I did about God, religion, and the afterlife. I should have been terrified, but Lucian was real in my hands. I trusted him implicitly. I could feel that we had always been connected.

"Do you want a drink?" I asked.

He shook his head. After a few seconds of silence and some deep breaths, he said, "I'm not going to let one little disintegrating feather ruin our day." He smiled, seeming satisfied, before closing his eyes again and nuzzling into my chest.

"Right," I said.

A moment later, his eyes shot open as he sat up quickly. "I just realized something."

"What?" I asked.

"I'm free. Fuck, let's do something. Let's go have sex in the shower and go eat and go to a movie and go dancing and walk through Golden Gate Park. Let's sail. Do you want to sail? What about bowling? Oh my God, I want to dance in the rain. I want to hold your hand on the trolley. Let's go to the Wharf and eat clam chowder. Let's take one of those shitty ferries to Alcatraz and then I'll fly us back. I'm only one feather short. You should see Zack's wings; seriously, it's amazing the guy can even get off the ground. I'll be fine. I feel like a million bucks. Evey, I feel alive!" He was excited, triumphant even, and talking a million miles an hour.

"I'll do anything you want. Do you want to meet my parents?" Why I had the urge to take Lucian to my parents' house, I'll never know, but it was a strong urge.

"Jane and Steve? Yeah, I know them well."

"But they don't know you."

"True. Let's go to Oakland to see your parents. After the shower sex though, okay?"

I kissed him on the nose. "Deal."

I called my mom and asked if we could come out for dinner. I told her I was bringing someone for them to meet. Thinking back to the conversation I had had with my parents earlier, she must have thought I was hesitant to introduce them.

"Is this the guy you told your father about?" she asked.

"What guy?" I said, forgetting momentarily that I had mentioned my date from the other night. "Oh yeah, sort of."

"Sort of?" There was no humor in my mother's voice.

"He's been a good friend for a while. You guys will like him. We just started dating."

"Okay, I'll make spaghetti. Will he like that?"

"I'm sure, Mom."

Lucian was already in the shower. "Get in here," he yelled.

I covered the mouthpiece of the phone and yelled back, "One second." I returned to my mother. "Mom, we'll be there in about an hour."

"Okay, honey. Love you."

When I left my room to head toward the bathroom, Brooklyn was leaning against the wall in the hall, staring me down. I scowled at her. "Mind your own business," I said before she could even get a word out.

"I'm just shocked is all. And I'm leaving, getting a bite with Cherry."

Cherry was the friend Brooklyn always tried to use to make me jealous. Brooklyn and I clearly had an unhealthy relationship, but I didn't care anymore, and I wasn't jealous of her friendship with Cherry. Cherry was a head case.

Inside the bathroom, I undressed. Unabashed, I stepped into the shower behind Lucian. He turned immediately and took me in his arms.

"Hello, beautiful," he said, and then his mouth was on my neck, and there was no more talking.

Shower sex isn't always easy or satisfying. It rarely is, actually, but with Lucian, it was pure bliss. I was weightless. Even after we were through, I felt like everything was perfect and right in the world. But how could it be, when what we were doing must have been breaking some cosmic law of the universe?

I wanted to crawl back into bed with him, but Lucian convinced me to get dressed. We walked to the BART. He was glancing all around, looking for something or looking at something. He grabbed my hand at one point and jerked me forcefully in a different direction.

"What's going on?" I asked.

"Nothing. I'm getting some strange looks. And I didn't see Zack or Abigail on my way out."

"Who's Abigail?"

"Brooklyn's poor excuse for an angel. It doesn't matter. Let's just get to your parents."

"Should we fly there?" I wiggled my eyebrows, excited over the idea.

"Probably not a good idea. We should try to blend in, lay low for a while until I can figure out what's going on."

On the BART he held me close as he braced the metal pole. The train car was full, and Lucian looked to be on high alert for some reason.

"I just want to get to your parents'," he kept saying.

"Are you worried you can't protect me anymore?"

"No, I can protect you." He stared into my eyes. "You're safe, okay?"

"Okay," I said, but I already knew that.

My parents lived in a small suburb of Oakland, in the same house I was born in. It was a modest tract home, but it was warm and always smelled like homemade food. My mother swung the door open before I could ring the doorbell.

"Hello," she said with a smile. Her attention was

immediately drawn to Lucian as he held out his hand.

"Hello, Ms. Casey, it's nice to meet you," Lucian said.

"Please call me Jane." She appraised him and seemed taken aback.

"Okay, Jane," he said as they continued shaking hands for what seemed like too long.

She turned on her heel and walked toward the hallway. "Come on in and meet Evey's dad."

In the hallway, I whispered, "Did you do something to her?"

"No, I swear."

"What was her deal? She acted odd."

He shrugged. "I have no idea why."

My father and Lucian had a similar introduction, then my mother offered Lucian a drink. He declined, and I was surprised.

"Is it all right if I have a glass of wine?" I asked him.

"Of course," he said, as if it were a silly question.

My mother pulled me into the small guest bathroom and shut the door.

"What are you doing?" I asked.

She was wearing a funny yellow apron that said *Sauce Boss* on it. I laughed at it, but she wasn't amused. My mother and I looked exactly alike in facial structure and body, but she had blond hair and blue eyes and I had dark hair and dark eyes like my father. Her eyebrows arched.

"Say something, Mother."

"What does he do for a living? He's older than you, right? Where did you meet him?"

"Geez, is this the Spanish inquisition? You don't like him?"

"Evey, he's gorgeous—I mean, exotically handsome, but I don't know him and this just seems a bit sudden. I'm just curious about him. Curious why you've never mentioned him, and you're already bringing him home to meet the parents."

"God, he really is good-looking, isn't he?" I said dreamily.

"Evelyn, focus."

"I've known him for a while. He's a bit older than me." What an understatement that was. "I met him through mutual friends. He's in securities."

"Securities?" My mom looked skeptical.

"Some kind of business with brokerage firms... something like that."

"So he works in the city? In an office?"

I hesitated. "Yes?"

"Is that a question, Evelyn?"

I was worried she'd walk straight out of the bathroom and ask Lucian about banking securities, which was exactly what she did. I tried to stop her. Lucian was sitting in the living room on the couch, talking about, of course, UPS delivery service.

My dad said, "Hey, DD, this guy is a serious history buff. He knows everything about the beginnings of the United Parcel Service."

"Yeah, Lucian's a reader," was all I could think to say.

Lucian was looking at me, wearing one of those smiles that made it hard not to smile back. He looked like a little boy about to walk into Disneyland.

"Lucian," my mother said.

"Yes, Jane?"

"So you're in banking, Evey tells me."

"Yes, that's right." I knew he'd pick up on what to do. "Asset securities to be exact." He winked. I lost my balance and had to grip the back of the couch.

"What are asset securities?" my father said.

Oh shit, what if he doesn't know?

"It's actually pretty simple. I buy shares in companies or in mutual funds that are invested in the stock market. It's a lot of number crunching. It's not that exciting, but it pays the bills."

God, he's good.

"Do you want to see my childhood bedroom, Lucian?" I asked.

"Evey," my mother scolded.

"Just to show him around," I whined.

My mother rolled her eyes. Lucian looked back at my dad for approval.

"Go ahead, DD, show him around."

"Come on." I grabbed Lucian's hand and pulled him down the hall to my bedroom. With my back to him, I said, "So this is it. I'm an only child." He laughed, so I turned on my heel. Our faces were inches apart. "Why are you laughing?"

"Because I know you're an only child. I've known you since you were a baby, remember?" He opened his eyes wide for emphasis. "I know a lot about you."

I had forgotten about that little fact. For a while, we had just been a couple of people getting to know each other. I knew I had a sour look on my face when Lucian added, "Not everything though. There's a lot I don't know about you."

"What don't you know about me?"

"I can't read your mind."

"Oh, big deal. So you don't know what I'm thinking? Most people can't read minds. How did you know I told my mom about the securities thing? We were whispering in the other room. By the way, are my parents' angels in here with us?"

"No, they're outside—two females. I've known them since you were born. They hang out on that old porch swing, smoking cigarettes... menthols. Your mom always thought your dad was sneaking cigarettes."

I laughed. I knew about that. I remember her accusing him once.

"They're usually really nice," he said, "but they gave me a dirty look when we walked up, so I didn't say anything." He clenched his teeth like the angels outside might be a problem.

"You never answered me. How'd you know what I told my mom if you can't read minds?"

"I can hear you from far away when you're speaking aloud. But I can't hear your thoughts. Sometimes when I'm worried about you"—his lips moved closer to mine—"I wish I could hear your thoughts, but other times, I'm glad you're a mystery to me."

I pecked him on the lips and pulled away. "I'm the mystery?"

His eyes moved to my mouth. "I don't understand anything anymore." He pulled my body flush with his. "I just know this feels right and good."

I believed Lucian was grappling with something far bigger than even my own disbelief of what was happening and what he was. I had always been of a very sound mind. There was never a time, even in my young childhood, when I imagined things that weren't there or made up stories in my head. Now I was kissing my guardian angel in my childhood bedroom in Oakland, and all I could think about was how badly I wanted him to put his hand up my shirt. That was where my head was at. In the gutter would be an understatement. Lucian knew he had that effect on me. He knew I would never be able to get him out of my system.

We finished an early dinner with my parents, then Lucian and I spent the rest of the evening running around town, doing the things Lucian said he had never been able to enjoy. We went bowling and drove go-carts and watched twenty minutes of a cheesy romantic comedy in an old theater. I couldn't even remember what it was about because we were basically making out in the back the whole time. He didn't do anything angel-like that night. We walked from the Wharf to Ghirardelli Square and shared a giant ice cream sundae. We were a normal couple.

Back at my apartment, I drank a glass of wine and Lucian had tea. We made smooth, sleepy love. It was effortless. It was blissful.

Brooklyn knocked on my door at two in the morning. I was sleeping, but of course Lucian was just lying there, perfectly still... watching me. The idea sounds unnerving, but he was always watching me, and so I became accustomed to it quickly.

"Brooklyn's at the door," he whispered.

I got up and pulled a blanket off the end of the bed to cover myself. "Hold on, Brooke."

When I got to the door and looked back, Lucian was sprawled on the bed without any modesty. I ran back over and covered him with the sheet. He just smirked at me.

"Oh, stop it," I said to him.

When I opened the door, Brooke scowled. "Geez, took you long enough."

"What's up? It's late. I have to work tomorrow."

She leaned to one side of me to peer into the room. I looked back to see Lucian wave to her and smile.

Near my ear, she said, "Was just making sure you were okay."

"That's the first time you've ever done that," I told her.

"That's not true." She was still trying to look around me, but I was blocking her.

"We're fine, thanks."

"What's up with you and him?" she asked.

"We're having mind-blowing sex in here, Brooklyn, can you leave us alone?" Lucian called out.

Her eyes widened.

"He's kidding," I said. "We were sleeping, and now we are going back to sleep and you are going to your room."

She shook her head. "Whatever. We'll talk later."

When I crawled back into bed with Lucian, he was pretending to be asleep, even fake snoring. I tickled him under the arms. He squirmed but kept his eyes closed. "You're ticklish," I teased. I was relentless until he literally begged me to stop.

"Please," he said, "I'll tell you anything you have ever wanted to know."

I stopped. "Anything?"

"Anything," he said.

"What was the one time you saw me naked? You mentioned that before."

He shut his eyes and took a deep breath through his nose and out of his mouth. "It was a couple of years ago. I was hanging out on your fireplace mantel, just bored. You and Brooklyn were getting ready to go out. Did I mention that I was bored?"

I rolled my eyes. "Go on."

"You called out something from the bathroom. I can't remember exactly what it was. You said you thought your breasts were crooked."

"I remember, keep going," I said, although I could tell he was tormented by something. As he went on, the story seemed to get harder and harder for him to tell.

"It was weird for me, Evey. I can't explain it."

"Try." With my index finger, I drew circles around the little smattering of hair on his chest.

"When you called out to Brooklyn about it, I heard her say something rude to herself about your breasts. You came walking down the hallway in a towel—you know how Brooke is jealous of you?"

"I don't think she's jealous of me."

"Yes, she is. That's why she's knocking on your door at two a.m. I knew she was going to be hurtful that day. I had witnessed it before, and you've always been so sweet to her."

It looked like he was getting emotional. I was too.

"What did you do, Lucian?"

"You were going to open your towel and show her, so I popped into her body just for a minute."

I remember that day well. I'd thought Brooklyn was out of her mind. She had said, "You're beautiful, Evey. You have a really nice body, and you should never feel insecure about it."

Lucian went on. "I got in trouble for that. I'm not supposed to protect your heart, but I didn't want to see you hurt by Brooklyn's words. And you were looking at me, just standing there completely naked, looking so pretty and vulnerable. It was selfish of me."

"No, it was selfless of you." I cupped his face with my hands and kissed him. "I love that you'd do that for me."

"You haven't heard the whole story. The worst part is that when I popped out of Brooklyn's body, I stood behind her, transfixed. I couldn't take my eyes off you." He laughed. "I got turned on. It was the first time I became really worried about what might happen between us. I took off and went and got a bottle. That's when I started drinking a lot more. I also got a serious scolding from Mona."

"Well, I'm glad I turned you on." I smiled.

He laughed once, but it seemed forced. Pulling my head down to rest on his chest, he said, "Go to sleep, Evey. I have some things to figure out tonight."

10

FEAR

Lucian

I HAD SOME time before magic hour to lie in bed and think while Evey slept peacefully on my chest. I had lost another feather earlier but hadn't mentioned it to her. I didn't want to worry her. I gently removed myself from her bed and went outside. I felt weak and thought maybe it was due to extreme alcohol withdrawals. Across the street, I spotted an angel where Zack normally sat.

"Hey," I said to him.

He flew onto the roof without responding.

Abigail was also nowhere to be found. I plopped down on the stoop until it was time to go find Mona. I flew slowly to the St. Francis soda shop and tried to open the door, but it was locked. I knocked, and then tried to pass through the glass but couldn't. All I could see around me were humans frozen in motion.

I went to the Star Wars bar, but no one was there.

Standing on the street, I called out, "Mona, Zack, Abigail, anyone?"

I flew toward the Golden Gate. It was raining pretty hard by then, but there were always angels on the bridge during magic hour. It was the best vantage point to see the sun piercing the horizon. About halfway to the bridge, I looked down and saw an angel struggling in the wind and rain. As I got closer, I noticed it was Zack. His wings had always been too weak for bad weather. I grabbed him from above to right him in the wind.

"What are you doing?" he screamed. "Take your hands off me, you traitor."

"No, Zack, listen."

"No!" His voice was a high-pitched screech.

"Just hear me out. You're my best friend," I shouted over the rushing wind. I directed us to Coit Tower to sit on the roof and talk.

"I don't want to be here," Zack said.

"Please just listen to me. I need to know what's going on. Am I banished? Why can't I find Mona? Please." I looked him in the eyes. "You're my only friend."

Compassion flooded his expression. "You're not banished."

That brightened me up. "I'm not?"

"Worse, I think."

"What?" I asked.

Hesitating, he said, "I don't know, Luc. They reassigned all of us, even Mona. They said we weren't to talk to you."

"Who is 'they'?"

"Some David guy, along with you-know-who."

"No, I don't know who."

Zack shrugged. "Your favorite person."

"Jesus? I love him, and he loves me. He loves everyone."

"You told me one time that you didn't get the hype. Now you're saying you love him?"

"We had a falling out a long time ago, but that's in the past. I got over it, and he should too. Isn't the forgiveness thing his whole schtick anyway? And by the way, that debacle with Mary Magdalene had nothing to do with me. I couldn't control her. I think he and I are on good terms now though."

"You're always saying that, Luc. It was a long time ago, but you still haven't taken responsibility for it. I think that's the only thing causing problems for you now."

"No, what's causing problems for me now is that I'm in love with Evey. My past wouldn't be an issue if it weren't for her. Why didn't they banish me to the Star Wars bar?"

"Because of your past. They've just had it. They think you're a lost cause."

"A lost cause? Do you know how many great events in history I'm responsible for?"

"I gotta go," Zack said.

"You're my best friend, Zack." *If I said it enough, maybe he'd believe me and stick by me.*

"I have to go and do what's right." He reached his hand out for a shake, and I pulled him into a hug.

"I'm going to miss you," I told him.

"It might not be forever."

"I hope not, but I'm changing. Something is happening to me." He nodded but didn't reply. "Zack, will you please find

Mona and tell her I need to talk to her?"

"I'll see what I can do." Then with complete sorrow written on his face, he flew away into the powerful wind, flapping his crappy wings as hard as he could to get enough lift.

I got a chill sitting on top of the tower. I had never been cold before. Wrapping my wings around myself, I waited. There was a thump behind me... feet landing.

"Lucian?" Mona sounded defeated.

I couldn't look at her. I kept my head down when I spoke. "How bad is it?"

"I fought for you."

"Just tell me how bad it is." *What is everyone keeping from me?*

"All the higher-ups decided you weren't worth helping."

She was standing next to me by that point; I could feel it. "So I'm not banished, but it's worse? I lost two feathers today."

"That's going to happen."

"What else is going to happen, Mona?"

"I'm not certain, but I don't think it will be pretty."

I looked up into her eyes for the first time since she had gotten there. "She'll be crushed if anything happens to me. This will ruin Evey. It will break her heart into a million pieces. She'll never be the same. I'll stop seeing her if I have to. I'll erase her memory. You can reassign me."

"I think it's too late for that."

"I don't understand. What's going to happen? Tell me, please. What? Poof? No, please tell that's not going to happen." I was pleading not for my own life but for Evey's sake. "She'll die. She's in love with me." I knew my eyes were as wide as saucers.

"I don't know what will happen, but if it is poof, she won't remember you at all. You'll be forgotten."

Anger boiled over in me. "Just like that, huh? And there's no stopping it?"

"Just like that."

"Please talk to the big guy for me. Do something. I promise I'll change. I already quit drinking."

"I don't think I can help, but I'll give it one last try, Lucian. And it's not just about quitting the booze. It probably has to do with you atoning for what you've done and asking those you've hurt for forgiveness."

"Atonement? Who have I hurt?"

"You've hurt Evey." Hearing that felt like a stake in the heart. "Lucian, you've interfered with her life in such a colossal way there is probably no repairing it."

I shook my head. "There are always second chances."

"Not always. I know how well meaning you've always been. You looked out for her, but you just got too damn close."

"Anything you can do, Mona, I'm begging you."

She looked at her watch. "You have a minute or so to get back to her. And remember, as long as you're there, no one else will be assigned to her."

She was basically saying I was still responsible for Evey. Not that I would ever let anything happen to her, but I noticed I was a little slower to get off the ground from the top of Coit. I wondered if I was not only cursing Evey's heart, but her life too.

I made it back to Evey's just as magic hour was ending. She stirred, so I stripped down, crawled underneath the covers, and began kissing her belly. I thought about having a baby with her, knowing it was impossible. My eyes welled up from the idea that I was taking that away from her. I thought maybe I should just walk in front of a bus and end it all right there. Evey would forget about me, and I would disintegrate into nothingness.

"Oh, Lucian," she moaned.

I moved down farther until I was kissing her there. She tasted so good, and she was making perfect sounds and holding my head to her body, writhing beneath me, and that's when the whole bus idea started sounding really bad.

I sat up on my knees. "Turn around."

She did. She got on her hands and knees, totally exposed to me. I ran my hand down her perfect ass, and then I was inside her. Her back arched. She lifted off her hands and leaned into my body. We moved like that for a long time. Evey was out of her mind with lust. I could feel her heart racing and her legs trembling. She was crumbling all around me, coming with unrepentant joy. But for me, the guilt was eating away at my insides, and it was hard to stay in the moment.

"God, yes," she whispered.

When Evey was done, she plopped onto the bed, turned, and said, "Is something wrong?" She had sensed that I wasn't fully present.

I lay down beside her and took her in my arms. "No."

"You seemed far away."

"I just wanted you to feel good." I told her the truth, but she was right—I was far away. What Mona had said was a lot to digest. Why hadn't they just banished me? Not knowing what was going to happen would be my punishment?

Evey propped herself on her elbow and looked me in the eyes. "Are you sure?"

I nodded. "Positive. You know what?" I traced a line under her arm with my index finger.

She giggled. "What?"

"You need to get ready for work, young lady."

She rolled off me and looked up at the ceiling. "Ugh, Tracey."

"I know, I agree. She's unbearable."

"Isn't she? She's so full of herself."

"Just stick it out a little longer. She knows the right people."

"You're the first person who has told me to wait it out with Tracey. But you're right—it's the only sensible thing to do. Everyone is always saying I should ditch her."

"I have your best interest in mind. I'm not always going to tell you what you want to hear."

"I get that." She leaned in and kissed me. "I like your honesty." She reached behind me, and then with a grim look, she handed me a feather. "Another one."

When I reached for it, it disintegrated. *Jesus, really? This is how it's gonna be?*

"Why don't you ride in the car with me?" she suggested, pulling me out of my head.

"Okay."

On the way to work, I had to tell Evey to slow down twenty times. She drives like a maniac. That driving instructor she'd had when she was sixteen was terrible. If I hadn't had intervened, she'd be dead by now.

"Don't be a backseat driver," she said.

"I taught you better than this."

"You didn't teach me; my dad taught me."

"I became your driving instructor after the first lesson when I realized Mr. Willis didn't know what he was doing. I became him for your behind-the-wheel lessons."

"What?" She looked shocked. "You put your hand on my leg and squeezed it during the last session. I thought he was a total perv."

"I did not!"

"You did too!" She looked at me pointedly.

"Eyes on the road, Evey."

When we got to the warehouse, I said, "I'll just sit in here and be invisible."

"Won't you be bored?"

I laughed hysterically. "This is what I've always done, and yeah, it's boring as fuck."

"Come in with me. Meet Tracey for real. She'll love you. You have a perfect body for design."

I frowned. "I'm not letting her dress me up."

"Then let me."

We walked in through the large roll-up door. There were tables and material scraps everywhere, and in the corner was a huge roll of denim. Tracey was talking to another assistant, who scurried away when Evey and I came in.

"Who's this beautiful man?" Tracey said while she stared me up and down.

"This is my boyfriend, Lucian."

"He's *your* boyfriend?" she asked with more shock than spite.

"Yes," Evey said, "he's *my* boyfriend."

Tracey wasn't unlike Brooklyn in that she would probably be forever single, but she didn't want to be. That was the difference. She was aging fast, approaching her mid-forties, and still had no serious male prospects. Part of the reason was that she emasculated and objectified men in a really disgusting way, much like she was doing to me presently.

"Take off your shirt," she said to me.

"Excuse me?"

"Are you shy or something? You got little boy chest under that tee?"

I was still me, okay? I couldn't resist. I pulled off my T-shirt and threw it to the side. I had left my belt and boxers at Evey's, so there wasn't much material left to hide anything. I didn't even bother pulling up my hanging jeans. They covered the important part.

"Jesus, lord," Tracey said. People really needed to stop saying that. I was starting to get a complex. She looked at Evey. "He's perfect. Perfect shoulder width, sculpted jaw and abs, narrow hips." She turned to me. "How tall are you? What's your inseam?"

"Six two. Maybe thirty-five inseam."

Evey came over and whispered in my ear, "You're eating this up."

"I have a plan," I whispered back. I knew which items Evey had designed, but to Tracey, it was my first time in the warehouse.

Tracey left and then came back over with a stack of jeans and some T-shirts. I really had no shame. When I dropped my jeans, Tracey and the assistant lurking behind her froze. They went slack-jawed.

Evey, standing next to me, looked over and said, "Really, Lucian?"

"Well, he's definitely not shy." Tracey approached Evey

and said, "How'd you land him?"

I slipped on a pair of jeans that I knew Tracey had designed because they were hideous. I shook my head, pulled them off, and dug around for a pair that Evey had worked on. "These are perfect."

"Evey, we have a photographer coming," Tracey said as she ran to the phone. "I'm canceling the other model. Lucian, how do you feel about making an easy grand?"

"Why not? But I only want to be photographed in these jeans." I pointed at Evey's.

Tracey was a ball-buster. "Well then, I better keep the other model on. Your pay just went down to two hundred."

"Fine by me," I said, although I wondered how I was going to get money now that I had been cut off from Mona and the higher-ups. *No, Lucian, you are not going to model Tracey's jeans.*

The photographer only took about four shots of me. I kept my head down as much as I could, wondering what would happen to the photograph after I was gone. Would it just go poof like the rest of me? Was that my fate?

After we were done, Evey pressed her warm hand to my cheek. Looking into my eyes, she said, "Thank you. She would have never photographed the other model in those jeans." I smiled but suddenly felt too weak to talk. "Are you okay, Lucian? You look pale."

"I need to eat. Low blood sugar."

"Oh yeah, you have that crazy metabolism," she said.

But the truth was that angels didn't need to eat. We *could* eat and enjoyed eating, but nothing happened if we didn't. I was feeling weak because I was getting sick or starving, something I had never experienced.

"Come on," I said, "let's go get lunch."

"Tracey, is it all right if I do some sketches at home and take the rest of the day off?"

"Two days in a row, huh?" Tracey asked.

I think both Evey and I had forgotten she'd missed the day before.

"I'll email you sketches tonight, I promise," Evey said.

Tracey quirked an eyebrow at me. "As long as he's the subject."

I rolled my eyes.

Once in the car, Evey asked where I wanted to go to lunch and I told her anywhere, so we ended up at her favorite Japanese restaurant. I had spent many Saturday nights hovering in the corner while Brooklyn and Evey drank sake with one random imbecile or another.

I felt a tiny bit better after eating, and I had no idea why. Back at Evey's apartment, Brooklyn was sitting on the couch when we walked in. She was still in college, on the ten-year plan. She spent most days on the couch, surrounded by a pile of books I knew she hadn't read. Studying, she called it. Her parents pretty much supported her and probably would for the rest of her life.

"Hey guys," she said. "Do we need to start charging you rent, Lucian?"

"He's not feeling well, Brooke. He's gonna go lie down for a bit in my room while I work on some sketches."

"Oh, right, I'm sure that's what you guys will be doing."

"Shut up, Brooklyn," I blurted.

She turned around to look at me. "What is your problem, weirdo?"

I kept forgetting that she had only just met me. "Nothing, I'm sorry. I'm really cranky."

"Come on," Evey said as she pulled me down the hall.

11

TIME
Evelyn

I WAS SKETCHING on the small drafting table in my bedroom while Lucian rested on the bed. My mind was somewhere else. I had spent an hour sketching and had nothing to show for it but a pile of crumbled up papers at my feet. I couldn't focus. All I could think about was how strangely Lucian was acting. I had to remind myself that he was an angel and this was uncharted territory. I wondered at what point I would start to freak out. How was I so accepting of this reality?

I looked at him and noticed his eyes were closed. "Lucian?"

He didn't move. When I sat on the edge of the bed, he stirred before opening his eyes. He blinked a few times and then opened his eyes very wide. "I just fell asleep," he said, in shock.

"Weird. Does this mean you're becoming a human?" My voice was hopeful.

"I don't know. I have to find Mona tonight." He kept saying that, but nothing seemed to be getting answered. He stood and spread his massive wings while laughing. I couldn't tell if he was shocked or excited about the fact that he had fallen asleep. "Well, those are still there. That's good, I guess," he said.

"Don't you want to be human, Lucian?"

He stared at me for several long seconds. "I don't think that's how it works. I'm going to have to find out more info." He focused his attention on the bed then laughed again.

"What?" I said.

"I had a dream. It was so strange."

I fully expected him to tell me about a dream that would reveal something really important, but he just continued to laugh. He buckled over, holding his hand to his stomach. I could no longer see his wings, and he just looked like an average guy, standing there in a fit of uncontrollable laughter. Above average guy, I should say.

"Tell me about it, Lucian."

"I think it was actually a nightmare, but it was hilarious."

"Oh no, what was it?" I asked.

"I was being chased, then I got eaten by a giant chocolate chip cookie."

"What? That's really dumb."

When he fell onto the bed laughing, I joined him in the hysteria. He tried to calm down but was still chuckling when he said, "I was actually really scared. Dreams are weird." He was experiencing the world anew.

"So that's the first one you've ever had?"

"Yes. How can you humans handle being part of something that is completely out of your control? I couldn't even control my own body."

"Well, it's not real, obviously. Otherwise, you would have been eaten by a cookie and you wouldn't be lying here talking to me."

"No, I know." He turned on his side, cupped my cheek and ran his thumb over my lower lip. His eyes were fixated on my mouth. He looked thoughtful and curious. "I guess I'm still trying to figure things out. It's so confusing."

When I leaned in to kiss him, he rolled onto his back. I straddled his waist as he unbuttoned my shirt. Pushing it off my shoulders, he said, "I want to look at you."

"You've seen me."

He laughed. "I want permission to look at you."

I got up from the bed. "You saw me that night with Keith... or you saw me when you *were* Keith. And when you were Brooklyn that day. And you saw me last night and this morning."

"I did," he said, smiling serenely.

"That night after the concert... I'm not usually like that. I—"

"I know you're not, Evey. Come here."

I slowly undressed myself, and then stood next to the bed and removed Lucian's shirt and jeans. The whole time he watched me with an intensity I had never seen in a person. "You have full permission to look at me now," I told him.

"I'm literally dying to," he said, and it was as though a needle had gone coasting across the face of a record. He had put emphasis on the word *literally.*

"What?"

"Nothing," he whispered. "Come here."

"Are you being funny, or are you actually dying? Are you dying so that you can be with me? Is that the sacrifice?" Tears came rushing to my eyes. I was naked and vulnerable, confused and hurting. I had only just met him, but I had known him my whole life. There was so much comfort in being with a person who already knew all of my flaws, but his confession made me feel something I hadn't felt with him— fear. "Answer me."

"I don't know for sure," he replied.

"I'll cut my wrists." I had never said anything like that to anyone. I had never had a suicidal thought.

His eyes went wide. "Stop it, Evey! Don't say that. Anyway, there are better ways to go." He tried to make light of it. Tears went running down my cheeks. He pulled me onto the bed and held me. That familiar sensation of feeling safe and loved coursed through me. "I'm sorry. That wasn't funny," he said.

I started to cry full, quiet sobs. "I can't live without you."

"You just met me. I'm a terrible drunk. I'm a jerk. I'm a womanizer."

"That's not going to work on me. I know what you're trying to do," I told him in a strong voice. "You have to take me. You have to take my life." I couldn't believe what I was saying. Would I really die for him? I guess I trusted I would be with him if I did.

He stood and covered me with the blanket. "Don't move. I need to do something."

"Don't leave. You said you wouldn't leave."

He stood in the middle of the room and looked up at the ceiling. "God, do you see this? God, do you see what's happening to Evey?" Lucian still focused on the ceiling, nodded as though someone was talking to him. "I know she's out of her mind. She doesn't realize it won't work. I know, God. I have to leave her alone. I know what I have to do."

"You're a liar!" I got up, held the blanket to my body and pointed at him. "You're lying. You said you don't talk to him and he doesn't talk to you."

"Evey, please calm down." He was sweating. I'd never seen him sweat.

"I think *you* need to calm down." He swayed and gripped the table next to him to steady himself. "Lie down with me, Lucian. You don't look well."

"I can't handle you talking the way you were talking."

I saw the fear in his eyes. "I'm sorry, I won't do it again," I told him.

He stumbled back to the bed and pulled me down with him. We wrapped ourselves around one another, legs and arms and mouths. I didn't know anymore where I ended and he began. We were lost in each other. The truth of what was happening was too much for us to think about. All we could do was try to comfort one another.

We dozed off at four in the afternoon. Around six, I got up and left a sleeping Lucian, so I could go into the kitchen and make lunch for us. When I came back with a turkey sandwich on a plate, he groggily opened his eyes and smiled.

I held out the plate. "Hungry?"

He eyed the sandwich for a moment before slowly taking the plate from my hands. "Thank you, Evelyn." He wasn't used to someone taking care of him.

"How are you feeling?"

"A lot better. I guess after a couple of thousand years, I was due for a little nap."

"Are we going to talk about what happened earlier?" I said.

He held the sandwich out to me, smiling. "Bite?"

I shook my head. "Don't try to change the subject."

"I don't want you talking about killing yourself ever again." His tone was unwavering. "I don't know what's happening. I'll find out more. But for now, I want to enjoy every minute I have with you."

"Because you don't know how much time we have?" I asked.

"Because no one knows how much time they have, and I am in love with you and I want to love you right now, Evey, no matter what happens."

It was time to change the subject. The unknown was too terrifying to ponder for any length of time. I wiped mustard from his beautiful lip. "Eat your sandwich. Maybe we can catch a movie after this."

He smiled. "No chick flicks though. I went from being forced to watch kid movies to teen angst to chick flicks. I want to see a thriller or one of those superhero movies."

I rolled my eyes, laughing. My sweet Lucian, like a little boy. He'd been subjected to everything I had wanted to do for so long. He was finally getting a chance to make some decisions, and I loved watching him experience that freedom. "Anything you want," I said. His face lit up.

I found another feather on the floor of my bedroom that day but didn't mention it to him. As I picked it up, it turned to dust in my hand. I wondered if that was eventually what was to come for him.

IN THE CAR, on the way to the movies, Lucian drove, and it felt like we were normal people going on a date.

"Can I ask you something without you getting upset?"

"Sure," he said.

"If you kill me, I'll become like you and everything will be okay?"

"I don't know, Evey. That's just what I heard from Zack. Half the time, he's full of shit. If I die, you won't remember me. I will be forgotten, and you'll go on with your life and get a new angel that doesn't break all the rules. You'll find someone to marry. A normal man," he said, in a low voice. "You'll have babies." He glanced over at me and smiled, but his eyes were full of pain. "Your fashion line will take off, and everything will be great. You're a good person. I have faith that good things will happen for you."

"But I want *you*, Lucian. No one else." I perked up and tried to lighten the mood. "I have my own theory about what's happening to you."

"What's that?"

"I think you're becoming like me... human."

"Maybe," he said absently. "Naps and food—I'm like a regular guy, aren't I?"

"Way hotter though," I said, and we laughed.

12

LIFE

Lucian

EVEN THOUGH I wanted to crawl into bed with Evey and sleep the night away, I knew I had to get more answers. I set up a fake Tinder account with a picture that blocked out my face but showed my shirtless body. I swiped right on Abigail's picture and waited. She responded. We planned to meet in room 212 at the St. Francis.

During magic hour, I rushed to the hotel, hoping to get into the room before her; otherwise, I was sure she wouldn't open the door. When she knocked, I swung the door open, yanked on her arm, and pulled her inside.

"Oh, you," she barked.

"Just shut it. I need to talk to you. I need some help."

"You look like shit."

I rolled my eyes. "Thanks."

"Why should I help you?"

"Because I've never done anything to you. But I did cover for you when you needed it, and I saved Brooklyn's life that one time she was drunk and hanging off the edge of a balcony like an idiot. You were nowhere in sight. You owe me."

"You seem sober for once."

"I haven't had a drink in days."

"I'm shocked, seriously," she said. "What do you want my help with?"

"It seems like you know things, like inside things."

"Well, I've been around longer than you have."

I pointed from her chest to mine. "You're older than me?"

"Duh." She twirled around. "Look at me. I'm a way better version."

I shook my head. "Whatever. I just need to know how I can be with her. Something is happening to me. I think I'm dying. Evey thinks maybe I'm becoming a human."

For the first time in the twenty-five years I had known Abigail, I saw compassion in her eyes. "I wish I could help you. I really do. You can be with her if you take her out— that's what I've heard. But there are consequences. I mean, do you realize what killing your own soul would mean? True blasphemy, sacrilege, all of that stuff."

"Zack heard a story about an angel in Memphis who drowned her soul and now they're together."

She shook her head. "I've heard that story, but I doubt it's all true. Anyway, why would you want her to become one of us now? Those new versions are a bit janky, you know?"

They really weren't, but old angels, even me, liked to pretend that we were so much better. If Evey became one of us, she wouldn't be herself anymore. Everything we'd shared would be gone. If I had been a normal man who had become an angel, I had no memory of my human life at all. She wouldn't either.

"I wish I could get some answers. Mona knows nothing," I said.

Abigail arched her thin eyebrows. "No one does."

"Why?"

"I don't know. We're just supposed to do the right thing and have faith that everything will work out." She caressed my cheek with her thumb. I don't know why I let her.

"That ship has sailed, Abigail. I haven't been doing the right thing for a while now."

She moved closer to me. "I'm sorry. I know you're going through a lot."

"I don't know why it's possible that I'm in love with Evey. There has to be a reason."

"Maybe the booze is scrambling your brain."

"I told you, I quit drinking."

"Well, we're different. I don't understand how you can even be attracted to her. Humans smell gross, and they're just not good-looking. They're not like us. I think we can get you back, Lucian. I think I can remind you of what it's like to be with one of us."

She leaned up to kiss me, and I pushed her back. "No, stop! What are you doing?"

She scowled. "Geez, you really are fucked in the head."

"Did I not make it clear? I'm in love with her. The crazy kind of love that you and I have seen over and over... in them, not us. It's the rip-your-bleeding-heart-out-and-step-in-front-of-a-speeding-train kind of love. You know what I'm talking about."

She huffed. "Jesus, dramatic much? Duh, Lucian, you feel that way about Evey because you're built to protect her."

"I doubt you feel this kind of love for Brooklyn."

"Yes, I do. I was devastated when she got herpes."

I shook my head. "That's not what I mean. I love Evey so much it's selfish. I crave her touch. The way she looks at me... it's not the same. I've been around long enough to know that."

"Well, I don't know what to say. You're hopeless."

"I know. Believe me, I know."

After she left, I wandered the streets for the rest of magic hour and watched as angels scurried away from me like I was some kind of demon pariah. I went into a liquor store and stole a bottle of Scotch. The counter employee was human, so it was an easy grab. Back at Evey's apartment, I sat on the floor of her bedroom and drank myself silly.

When she woke up, she spotted me in the corner. I was smiling and probably looking as stupid as I felt.

"Oh, Lucian."

"I naah tha drunk," I said, shaking my head.

"Come here."

I stumbled over and collapsed into her arms. "I gonna be sober in no tine," I slurred just before passing out.

Sometime later, I woke up to Evey sitting on the bed next to me, holding toast. "You need to eat, and I need to go to work. Why don't you stay here and get some rest?"

I sat up quickly and leaned against the headboard. "I have to go with you."

"No, stay, I'll be fine."

"I don't think you understand. I can't be away from you," I said.

She smiled shyly. "You're sweet."

"No, I literally cannot be away from you, Evey; I'm your guardian angel."

"Ha..." She looked away curiously. "That's right. I keep forgetting."

AFTER THAT NIGHT, we chose to put all of the questions away in the cupboard for a while. We carried on like a couple in love, spending every minute together. However wrong it might have been, we were so lovesick it made our choice to go against the rules feel right. I'd make myself invisible while she was at work, but she knew I was there. I'd knock something over and she'd start giggling, and pretty soon, Tracey thought Evey was losing her mind. But Evey was creating the best designs of her life, and I was the happiest I'd ever been. I didn't tell Evey that I lost feathers every day and that things that used to be simple for me were getting harder and harder.

I found a weird and crappy way of making money. During magic hours, I'd go into heavy crime areas and steal from thieves. I'd take most of the money back to the rightful owners and keep a small share for myself. I didn't tell Evey; I wasn't exactly Robin Hood. I hadn't seen Zack in a long time. I did wish for a better life for him though. Maybe someday he'd give it all up for love like I had.

I caught Mona coming out of the soda shop one night, but she just held her hand up and said, "I can't. I'm sorry, Lucian."

Angels ignored me, God ignored me, I couldn't even get a retweet on Twitter... but at least I had Evey.

"THEY'RE OYSTERS, AND they're an aphrodisiac," I told her, lifting one to her mouth.

"I know what they are. I'm just not a fan. Plus, we don't need aphrodisiacs."

"True, but I always wanted you to have a sophisticated palate. You've never even tried an oyster. Just try it. If you don't like it, you don't have to eat anymore."

She laughed. "Sophisticated palate?"

"Yes. Jane and Steve were always feeding you Hamburger Helper and Shake 'n Bake chicken."

She scowled. "I hate it when you talk about my parents that way. And by the way, you're the one acting like a dad now."

"I love your parents, Evey; they made you." It was true. I owed them everything. "I'm just saying I want to give you life experiences you wouldn't have normally had. Here, try it."

She rolled her eyes but opened her mouth anyway. The oyster slid out of the shell onto her tongue. "Just one chomp then swallow it whole" She did. Her face scrunched up like it was the worst thing she had ever eaten. She gagged, her eyes watered, and then she finally gulped it down. "Good girl," I told her.

She glared at me. "That was disgusting."

"It's kind of an acquired taste."

"I don't want to acquire that taste."

I kissed her and tasted the salt water on her lips. "Mm, that's good," I murmured against her mouth. She deepened the kiss for a moment but then pulled away and squinted. "What?" I said.

"I didn't like the oyster at all, but that kiss was strangely erotic."

"I told you. I've been around for a while. I know these things. Plus, you wouldn't have had that experience with your dad." I wiggled my eyebrows at her.

Her expression fell. "How many women have you been with?"

"You're the only human I've ever been with." I smiled, satisfied with myself.

"No. You know what I mean."

"Oh, did you mean angels?"

"Yes, which is even worse, but tell me... how many?" She was getting jealous. I know it's weird, but I kind of liked it.

We were in the back of the Ferry Building, at an oyster bar that looked out at the bay. I scanned the bay for flying angels but didn't see any. "I don't know. It's been two thousand years. I've lost count."

She looked a bit disturbed but also thoughtful. "Let's just say for the sake of this argument, you've slept with five thousand angels."

I snorted.

"You jerk. I'm trying to make a point. I'm also trying to get to know you."

"You know me better than anyone, but five thousand? Come on. That would be less than three a year. Let's be realistic."

She squinted. "Give me a number, Lucian."

"Maybe... a few hundred thousand." I was being conservative. I shrugged. "There isn't much to do during magic hours. I'm not proud of it, okay?"

She put her head in her hands and groaned. I wrapped my arm around her shoulder.

"I bet I'm terrible in bed," she said, "compared to all the experienced women you've been with."

"Angels, they're different, and anyway, are you kidding me? It is out of this world, utterly spectacular with you. There's nothing else like it. We were made for each other, Evey. I believe that."

She looked up and smiled before lifting an oyster to my mouth. I swallowed it, and we kissed. "We should go home," she whispered near my ear.

We couldn't keep our hands off of each other long enough to finish a meal. On our way out of the Ferry Building I asked, "Hey, do you know how holy water is made?"

"Yeah, it's blessed by a priest, right?"

"Guess again, sweetheart."

"I don't know," she said, "tell me."

Leading her by the hand, toward the street, I turned back and grinned. "You have to boil the hell out of it."

She laughed all the way home.

LATER THAT NIGHT, sitting behind Evey in the tub, I washed and rinsed out her hair with water that I most certainly had blessed. She sighed with pleasure, and then said, "So what is it exactly, between you and me?"

In my most definitive and certain voice, I replied, "It's simple, we're in love."

"Right, but what does that mean? Will you just hover around me and have sex with me until I die?"

"Sounds perfect," I said.

She giggled. "You know what I mean."

"I do." I kissed the top of her head and then let my hand slide down her back until I reached her butt. She made a satisfied sound, so I pinched it.

"Ouch!" She squirmed away.

Brooklyn banged loudly on the door as she walked by. Her jealousy was off the charts. I picked Evey up out of the tub, grabbed a towel with my teeth, and carried her to the bedroom, both of us completely naked. I knew Brooke would love that.

After we dried off and slid into bed, I rolled over on top of Evey, pinning her between my arms. I kissed her nose. She tried to squirm out from underneath me, but I held her tight until finally, she started tickling me and I had to relent. She managed to roll us over until she was on top.

With one long stroke of her tongue, she licked a streak right up the side of my cheek while holding my hands above my head. "How's my oyster breath?"

"Divine." I kissed her on the mouth and rolled her back to my side. "Now go to sleep, my angel; it's late."

She mock pouted but curled into the crook of my arm anyway and dozed off moments later.

I knew exactly what Evey needed. I had always known what she needed; I was made to know. She needed normalcy. I feared I wouldn't be able to give her that forever, but there was no way I'd let someone stop me from trying, not Mona, not Zack, not even God.

IT WAS A Wednesday when I got down on one knee at that sketchy Japanese place Evey loved near the Wharf. "Marry me. I want to be your husband. I want you to be my wife."

"Yes," she had said breathlessly.

Later that night, we had a long talk.

"Why though, Lucian? Why are we doing it? It just seems so fast."

"You said yes, Evey. You said it without hesitation."

"Because I've dreamt about that moment my entire life and…"

I knew she had. She went through a phase when she was ten where she only sketched wedding dresses. She used to scour wedding magazines and create elaborate wedding ceremonies with Barbie dolls. I wanted her to have all of that. The guilt I felt for what I was doing to her was sometimes so unbearable that I'd become grumpy and despondent. All I could do was try to give her the things I knew she wanted.

It wasn't until she and Brooklyn got older that Evey forgot about those dreams and started dating all of those rejects. That was when she lost faith in love. Now her faith was strong, and she deserved the fairy tale.

"And so you said yes, but now you're having second thoughts?"

"I just don't know if I see the point," she said.

"I want you to have a wedding, and since you've stubbornly insisted on being with me, I'm going to do everything I can to create some semblance of normalcy for you. You've always wanted this. I know that about you. Plus, I already asked your dad for permission."

She sat up quickly and pressed her back against the headboard. "What? He must have been shocked. We've only been together for a couple of months."

"Nope, not shocked. I believe his exact words were, 'I've never seen my DD so happy. You have my most genuine blessing.'"

She laughed. "You're a charmer, you know that? You've already won my dad over, and my mother basically can't take her eyes off you, which I find a little disturbing. What am I going to do with you?"

"Marry me. You'll be my wife. I'll be your husband. Done." It surprised me how badly I wanted to be married to Evey. Such a human feeling.

She shimmied down and cupped my face. "Yes again, Lucian. Yes, I will marry you."

We kissed and kissed, and then I told her that I would never be able to give her babies.

She replied, "We can adopt a little angel who needs a home."

That was Evey... selfless. Why couldn't I be more like her?

As our wedding approached, Evey became swept up in plans with her mother and Brooklyn while I went unnoticed in the corner. The story that I was "at work" made me laugh every time I heard Evey say it. It also made me wish that I was a normal man who went to work and didn't linger somewhere out of sight.

I tweeted at Jesus, but he never responded. He had a secret account we all knew about. It was like our version of a confessional. He didn't ask me to repent though, so I guess I was forgiven, or maybe forgotten. Maybe a lot of us are forgotten. What happens when people stop doing their job? An angel dies and what if Mona forgets to reassign the soul? Mona is flawed too. I've seen her make mistakes. Are those souls forgotten just like me?

All I could do was focus on the present by making Evey the happiest bride in the world, but I feared what was to come. I had stopped showing Evey my wings—they were deteriorating. Maybe I was becoming a simple man. I thanked God in advance if that was true.

13

HOLY MATRIMONY

Evelyn

"YOU ARE ONE heck of a beautiful bride, DD... just like your mother. Are you nervous?"

"Not at all." It was true. I was marrying Lucian, so why would I be nervous?

It's practically impossible to hide your wedding dress from someone who pretty much hears and sees everything, but we managed to pull it off. No one had a clue as to what Lucian really was and it would always have to be that way.

One night, a few weeks after we got engaged, Lucian had asked me if I wanted a traditional wedding in a church. We had both laughed at the idea. I'd told him I'd be too worried he'd go up in a plume of smoke after stepping foot inside the house of God. He said the Earth itself was the house of God.

That made perfect sense to me.

Our outdoor wedding venue was small and intimate—basically a glorified back patio covered in twinkle lights and lush greenery on the other side of the bridge—just out of earshot of the bustling city. It was at the Outdoor Art Club in Mill Valley, surrounded by beautiful redwoods. There were farm tables and candles, and we'd gotten plenty of wine to go around. Even Lucian was planning to have some wine. Thankfully, bottles of whiskey were a thing of the past for him. He'd said it was easy to give it up after that last time he got drunk.

Our wedding site was a breathtaking scene, and Lucian had set the whole thing up.

I looked out at the ceremony space, fearing the seats on the groom's side would be empty, but to my surprise, they were all full. I was curious who all the people were. When he had told me before that he'd find a best man, I thought maybe Lucian was going to pay a bunch of actors to sit in as friends for him. We had already explained to my friends and parents that Lucian had no family, being an only child whose parents had passed away in a car accident.

Through a trellis, I saw Lucian standing under an arbor, wearing a suit and looking as handsome as ever. He was waiting for the ceremony to begin. Next to him stood his best man, a guy I had never seen before.

"Don't let him see you," my father said.

"He's not going to see me," I replied, knowing Lucian could hear me, even several yards away. I saw a smile playing on his beautiful lips.

"Let's get this show on the road," came Brooklyn's voice.

Off to the left, an acoustic guitarist and singer began

playing "Til Kingdom Come" by Coldplay. Lucian had chosen all the music. It was perfect.

"Don't start crying yet," my father said. "We have to walk down the aisle, DD."

"Let's do this," I told him.

The moment I turned the corner, I saw Lucian's mouth drop open. My dress was a simple A-line ivory and lace, something I had designed as a teenager. I was walking slowly, watching Lucian's expression. It was pure joy and wonder.

When we reached the end of the aisle, Lucian took my hand from my father's and said, "Hello." His smooth voice sent a chill down my spine. I could have melted into him right then and there in front of everyone.

"Hello," I said back.

"You are stunning, Evelyn. I'm the happiest man alive."

And just like that, we were two regular people, young, in love, and about to commit the rest of our lives to each other.

We finished with *Till death do us part* before kissing then turning and facing the crowd. His entire section was remarkably good-looking.

He leaned in toward my ear, laughing, and said, "Jesus forgives. It's kind of his thing." I wasn't sure what he meant but figured he'd fill me in later. Lucian and I danced the night away, swept up in each other and happy to see people sharing our joy. My parents were beaming, and Brooklyn was hitting on Zack, Lucian's best man, who I figured was not of this world either. Not nearly as good-looking as Lucian, Zack still had a glow about him. I think he was pretty flattered that Brooke was all over him, but he wasn't exactly reciprocating.

Lucian had told me once before that Zack was a rule-follower.

After the reception, a car drove us to a bed-and-breakfast near Napa. Our plan was to go wine tasting the following day. "You know I'm the best winemaker around," Lucian said, nibbling on my ear.

I spotted the driver eyeing us in the rearview mirror and giggled. "Stop. Let's wait until we get there." Lucian obeyed with a mock frown. "So tell me, who were all those people at the wedding on your side?"

"Angels," he said quietly. He grinned. "Zack really is my best friend, and Mona, the liaison, was there too. A bunch of them got their shifts covered to come and support me... support us. Although, I think it was more out of curiosity."

"What do you mean?"

"Well, you and I are a bit of a spectacle to them." I frowned at him, but didn't respond. He continued, "I mean they all seemed happy for us, but an angel falling for a human and marrying her doesn't exactly happen every day."

"That's a bit elitist, don't you think?"

"Angels can be obnoxiously self-righteous."

"Don't I know it." I laughed.

"I'm not like that anymore, Evey, obviously. Not since you," he said while running his hand up my thigh.

There is no doubt that Lucian's hand on any woman's thigh would make her fall speechless. "Mm," was my only reply.

"I guess they all got permission from the higher-ups, one last little way of saying good-bye," he said.

"Wait what?" My brain was back. "What do you mean good-bye?" I felt my heart begin to race.

"They are going to have to cut ties for good, I think."

"Because you're becoming a human?" I asked with wide, hopeful eyes.

He took my hand and squeezed it. That warm feeling coursed through me. "I don't know yet what's happening, but I don't want to think about it on our wedding night."

I felt as though Lucian was keeping something from me.

Once inside our wedding suite, he took his time undressing me until I was standing in nothing but a white slip. He shrugged his jacket from his arms and frantically kicked off his shoes.

"God, she is beautiful."

I couldn't tell if he was talking to me or directly to God. It didn't matter. I loosened his tie and began unbuttoning his shirt. He kissed a path down the center of my chest and took my nipple into his mouth through the slip, sucking on the silk and skin and making me crazy.

"Lucian, come up here, let me undress you."

"Not yet," he mumbled.

He dropped to his knees and pushed the silk slip up my thighs and began kissing me down below. I was losing my ability to stand. Bracing the back of my legs, he kissed his way up my body.

"I want you now," I told him.

"Patience, Evey." He pulled the slip up over my head as he rose to his feet. Running a smooth index finger down the side of my breast, he shook his head and said, "I can't believe I get to have you this way."

I continued unbuttoning his shirt before undoing his belt and pushing his slacks down his thin hips. With a little finesse, I forced his boxer briefs down. We stood there, staring at each other, bold... unwavering. It wasn't a dream anymore. We were still and naked, like winter trees. His eyes scanned me slowly, his chest pumping in and out, then instinctively, I jumped into his arms, straddling his waist. We were frantic then. He pushed me against the wall, moving inside me while his mouth was on my neck, sucking and tugging at my skin. I kept my hands tangled in his hair as our breaths got heavier and heavier.

"I can't slow down, Evey," he said.

"Don't stop, Lucian."

I could feel him trying to get a grip, so human, so uncontrolled. He moved us to the bed and took a step back, then for a moment, we were apart. He climbed up and was inside of me again, moving slower this time with his calculated grace.

"I've always loved you," he said as he kissed my ear.

I could not form words. He pulled my hands above my head. I watched the flexing muscles in his abdomen as he moved inside me. I was lost in his eyes, this being who had watched over me, protected me, taught me things, cared for me, comforted me, loved me. Now he was making love to me, and he was the only one who could do it—who could make true, perfect love this way.

Closing my eyes from the tingles bursting through my body and between my legs, I arched my back as his thrusts became harder.

"Open your eyes, Evelyn. Let me look at you."

The moment I did, I felt our release everywhere. He collapsed on me, sweating, smelling perfectly male, and breathing with such pleasure and contentment. We stayed connected for a long time.

"I want to sleep tonight, like a normal person." Lucian had been sleeping occasionally, but not at all like a human.

"Then sleep." I stroked his hair.

His breathing evened out, and before long, I felt myself dozing off right alongside with him.

"Lucian," I said, just before we were about to fall asleep.

"Yes, my sweet wife."

"What's my last name?"

He let out a tired laugh. "I don't know. I guess we can make one up."

"How about we take mine?"

"Deal."

"My parents will wonder why," I said groggily. "But who cares?"

"Right. Who cares?"

A moment later, we were asleep.

IN THE MORNING, I woke to Lucian's head on my chest and his hand pulling my legs around him. He stopped and sat up on his knees. He cupped and kneaded my left breast, but not in a sexual way. His eyes were open, wide and weary.

"What is it, Lucian?"

His face scrunched up. He swallowed. It looked like he was going to cry. "No, God." He breathed hard as he looked at the ceiling.

I was already starting to cry. "What, Lucian?"

"I felt something. A lump."

I frantically kneaded my breast until I felt it—a small lump on the side, right near the bottom. "Oh. Oh no." I was stunned, slammed back into reality.

Lucian got up quickly and got dressed. "I'm taking you to a hospital right now."

"I don't have health insurance," I mumbled.

"It doesn't matter," he replied irritably.

He was rushing around the room, throwing our stuff in bags. I stopped him near the door and took his beautiful face in my hands. I leaned up on my toes and kissed him slowly. When I pulled away, he was shaking his head. "Please, relax. It's probably nothing. It's the day after our wedding," I told him.

He squinted, eyes full of pain. "This is my punishment."

"No, don't say that. We're in love, and everything will be fine." I kissed him again and tried to deepen the kiss, but he seemed far away.

"Get dressed, please, Evey. I want to take you to the doctor."

I pinched his nose. "If it's nothing, you're making this up to me."

"If it's nothing, Evey, I'll fly you to the fucking moon."

"Really? Can you do that?"

"No, I can't do that. Don't be silly. There's no atmosphere."

I was laughing, but he was serious. "Lighten up, grumpy," I said, knowing there was nothing we could do in that moment.

"If it's nothing and I'm overreacting, I will do anything you want. I'd do anything you want anyway, but we are going get it checked out right now."

14

SOUL THAT SINNETH

Lucian

WHAT'S THE DEAL with the medical system? We sat in the ER for four hours and were told three times that Evey's situation wasn't a medical emergency and to call her doctor, rather than continue waiting. I stood at the counter waiting, angry.

"Cancer isn't a medical emergency?" I shouted at the intake employee. "Are you kidding me? She could be dying."

"She needs tests," the clerk replied. "Tests that can be performed in a specialist's office... tomorrow."

"Fuck it all to hell!" I said. The clerk grimaced.

I took Evey by the hand and quickly led her to the car. It was her twelve-year-old Honda that sounded like a jet engine every time you started it. "You need a new car," I told her.

Evey hadn't said anything to me in a long time. I had an empty feeling inside. My heart ached. It was her—I was feeling her feelings. I glanced over as I drove and noticed that she was crying quietly. "Don't be scared, please."

"*You're* scaring me," she choked out.

"What? No. I'm sorry."

I pulled the car over into a strip mall parking lot, got out, and rushed around to the passenger side. After opening the door, I pulled her out and held her to my chest. Her body relaxed. I wrapped my wings around us, so we were cloaked.

She brushed the inside of my wing with her hand. "You've lost a lot more."

"It's okay. Don't worry about me. I'm okay."

She started crying again. "What's happening to us, Lucian?"

"I don't know yet. I'll find out, I promise. Let's get you home."

Brooklyn, shockingly, had given up the apartment to Evey and me a week before our wedding. She said she needed something with more space anyway. I carried Evey over the threshold, and that did earn me a smile. But once we were inside, I insisted she call the doctor.

"I have an appointment tomorrow," she said after she hung up. "Let's not think about it for now. Let's plan our honeymoon."

"Okay, but I'm going to look for Mona tonight and see if I can get some answers."

"Maybe it's nothing and it has nothing to do with you."

I blinked at her. She could have been right, but I wasn't convinced. Jesus forgives, but there are rules for a reason.

We spent the rest of the afternoon wrapped in a blanket,

watching movies. We watched *Dogma*, and I laughed through the entire thing. Evey was curious if any of it rang true, and sadly, I couldn't confirm or deny much except that I was positive Alanis Morissette was not God. She thought it was so strange that I knew nothing.

"I guess it's a need-to-know kind of thing."

"Well, you're real, so the rest of it must be true."

I nodded. "I am real. Jesus was a real man, and now he's one of us, sort of."

"Where is he?"

"He spends a lot of time in Milwaukee, for some reason."

Evey laughed hysterically. "Stop it."

"I'm serious. Got sick of the desert, I guess."

"Now I don't know if I can believe anything you say."

"You can trust me, Evey. I'm telling you the truth. I don't care about any of that other stuff. You're all I care about."

"Well, you should care about yourself too, you know."

"I used to... I think." The mood had gone from light to serious again in a second.

When she fell asleep, I went out to the stoop to see if I could find anyone. At magic hour, I walked the streets, seeing very few angels. I ran into Zina coming out of the St. Francis. She was kind.

"I heard you married her," she said.

"I did."

"And nothing's happened so far?"

"What? Like a bolt of lightning? No."

"Hmm. I don't know. God works in mysterious ways."

I chuckled. "Wow, Zina, you're beautiful, smart, and two thousand years old. I would expect a bit more out of you than that tired old cliché."

"Clichés are that for a reason. Take care of yourself." She kissed me on the cheek and then took off into the air.

I walked six blocks until I finally heard the undeniably squeaky voice belonging to Mona.

"Mona," I yelled into the sky.

"Up here," she called back.

I spotted her flying straight toward the top of the Transamerica building, so I followed her. We sat side by side, perched on a small ledge.

"Look at this city, Lucian, so still like this. Beautiful, isn't it?"

"It is."

"Were you looking for me?" she asked.

"Yes." I looked down at my fidgeting hands. "Evey found a lump in her breast."

She huffed. "Well, Lucian, humans go to the doctor to get those things checked out. That's the protocol. What do you think, that you can heal her? You're not a fucking healer."

She seemed so agitated. What did she know that I didn't?

"Calm down. Why are you so angry?"

She wasn't looking at me—she was staring out into the distance. "I'm angry because you're causing a lot of confusion. Honestly, I think Evey will be fine, but one never knows. Cancer is a human disease. It has nothing to do with us."

"I don't believe that."

"It's a fact, and one that I had confirmed earlier today."

"You've been keeping tabs on me, on us?" I asked.

"I overheard you in the apartment, talking about it."

"You care for me, don't you, Mona?"

She sighed. "Both of you. I care for both of you. I was told there would be consequences for you, but I don't know what they'll be. Your selfishness alone will cause Evey pain; I know that. And it will have nothing to do with cancer."

Thinking that I was causing Evey pain stung me deeply. "If this is all my fault, then why are you concerned?"

She took a long breath. "Because I've seen you with her. You are different, or she is different. You should have found a way to control it, but you didn't. I don't know if you were capable of staying away from her in that way, and that's why I pity you now."

"I wasn't capable of staying away from her, I promise you that. But I'm still feeling lost, and I probably always will. I only feel normal when I'm with her. I just have to have faith that she'll be okay."

Mona smiled peculiarly at me. "That's right—faith. But if she's not okay? Will you curse God because of it, Lucian?"

"Wouldn't you?"

She laughed through her nose. "You never learn."

I checked my phone and noticed magic hour was almost over. "I gotta go."

I took off into the fog, and boom! I was suddenly spinning out of control. I'd had a collision. A moment later, I hit the ground hard.

"Oh fuck, my back!"

An angel hovered over me. A big male. "Watch where you're going, dumbass!" He spit on me before taking off.

"Oww," I moaned. My wings, jaw, and elbow were bleeding. "Oh fuck." I got up and stumbled home because I couldn't get off the ground.

When I came into the apartment, Evey was awake. Magic hour had been over for some time. She gasped. "My God,

Lucian, what happened? Were you drinking?"

"Geez, you really don't trust me. It was foggy; I ran into some massive linebacker angel."

"Come into the bathroom. Let me clean you up." She wiped the blood from my wings and elbow and kissed the blood from my mouth. It was the kindest thing anyone had ever done for me.

"You're an angel," I told her, but she just shook her head. "What time is your appointment?"

She looked at the clock. "In three hours."

"Can we rest?"

She nodded. "Lucian, your wings don't look good."

"They'll heal. I just need to rest."

She woke me two hours later, and I was surprised to see that my elbow and jaw still had visible lacerations. Maybe healing would take more than rest. Evey put Neosporin on my jaw. I tried to tickle her while she was doing it. "What are you doing?" she said.

"It's been too long since you've smiled. It hurts me when you frown."

"Really, does it physically hurt, Lucian, because I'm very literal?" She was copying what I had said to her the first night we met.

"I can't believe you remember that."

"I remember everything," she said.

I had zapped Evey like any other soul I'd watched over in the past, but everything had stayed with her, or it had all come back. Why? Maybe after I was gone, she would remember me and be tormented. Or maybe I'd have to watch her die, and I'd be tormented. And then I realized, that is love. That is life. Brutal and beautiful all in the same.

My body ached as I drove her to the doctor's office. Once inside, they swept her away to another room to do a mammogram, ultrasound, a biopsy and blood tests, then they told us to come back in two days. The doctor confirmed that there was definitely swollen tissue in Evey's breast. I was sure something was terribly wrong and that it was my doing. I thought maybe it was the beginning of our time in hell, and that I was responsible.

We went home and slept. We were supposed to be on our honeymoon, but it didn't feel much like a honeymoon at all.

Surprisingly, the next day, the doctor called us in. She was an older woman, experienced, which should have given us some peace, but she wasn't warm. Evey and I needed warm. Dr. Smythe was the kind of doctor that didn't feel the need to smile at everyone all the time. She wore a gray, coifed bun and a pair of bifocals on a chain around her neck. No stethoscope.

She gave us a tight smile when she entered the exam room, and nonchalantly she said, "So you two were just married?"

"Yes, three days ago," Evey said.

"Do you want kids?" Dr. Smythe asked.

I had known this would happen. Evey had cancer, and the doctor was going to ask about freezing eggs and talk about chemo and send us to an oncologist. This was the end. This was going to be Evey's life because of me.

"Oh God," I said.

The doctor looked at Evey and jutted a thumb in my direction. "What's his deal?"

"He's nervous," Evey replied. "I am too. Can you just tell us what's going on?"

"Well, you don't have cancer, but you are pregnant. Good all around, I hope. Congratulations." She beamed, and then the room went black.

I passed out. I just passed out right there on the exam room floor. When the nurse waved smelling salts in my face, my eyes shot open.

Evey was staring down at me from the exam bed, looking worried. "Lucian, what happened?"

"First-time dads sometimes have this reaction," the nurse answered her.

I stood on shaky legs. "Can you give my wife and me a moment?" I thought it was the first time I had referred to her as my wife to another person. I felt a sense of pride and smiled, even though I still felt like I was going to fall over.

Evey was watching me cautiously. "Wait," Evey said to the doctor.

My smile faded when the reality sank in. I was an angel; she was a human. I couldn't get her pregnant. I was paranoid and curious as to whom my wife had been sleeping with.

"What, Evey?" I said rudely. "Why do you want them to wait?"

She jerked her head back, apparently surprised by my tone. Then it occurred to me that I was always with her, so her getting pregnant by someone else without my knowledge would be impossible. I got nervous again. The room started spinning.

She shook her head at me and scowled before directing her attention to the doctor. "What's the lump then?"

"Just a cyst," the doctor said. "The biopsy brought back nothing. If it doesn't clear up in a few weeks, we can have it removed, but it might make more sense to wait until after the baby's born."

The word *baby* and that was it, I was on the floor again.

"Geez, Lucian, get a grip!" Evey yelled.

When the doctor and nurse left the room, Evey jumped off the bed and came over to me. She helped me up and directed me to a chair in the corner. She crawled into my lap. "We're gonna have a baby."

She was smiling. Tears of happiness filled her eyes. I knew they were happy tears because I could feel it in my heart. But I was shaking, still in disbelief. "It's impossible, Evey."

"I didn't think angels were possible either," she whispered near my ear.

"But you're so young, and your career..."

"Lucian, I'm starting to get the annoying feeling that you don't want this."

"I do want this, more than anything. I just can't believe it," I said.

"Do you have to see it to believe it?"

I just stared at her for several long moments, then I shook my head.

After we called the doctor back in, they calculated that Evey was very newly pregnant, about six weeks. Evey was paranoid about the six ounces of wine she'd had at the wedding, but I assured her that I'd been around long enough to know a few ounces of wine would be harmless. Back in the day, women drank wine like it was water during their pregnancies.

In the car on the way home, Evey said, "We need to figure out a way to make our situation more normal."

"What do you mean?"

"We can't spend every waking moment together anymore, Lucian."

"Excuse me? I don't think you understand." I turned and looked her in the eye. "Wait a minute, are you getting sick of me?"

"No, I love being with you."

"Well, I'd hope so, because we just got married and we're gonna have a baby."

"I just don't understand how this is going to work. Are you just going to be hovering around me all the time and while I'm in the bathroom for the rest of my life?"

"I don't hover around you. I give you space. And I've never gone into the bathroom when you were in there unless you asked me to." I raised my eyebrows at her.

"If giving me space means going outside for a few minutes, then you're crazy. You need a job and a hobby," she said.

"You're being irrational," I told her, even though Zack had basically said the same thing to me once. "If I'm not with you, you'll be alone."

"I can be alone! You said yourself you had a light caseload. Other angels cannot be in two places at once, so how do they manage more than one person?"

I was getting more and more frustrated by the second. "That's when bad stuff happens. Do you want bad stuff to happen to you?"

"We'll have to take our chances sometimes."

I was quiet, trying to process what she was saying, trying to process the fact that she was carrying my baby and wanting more freedom from me at the same time. Since the moment Evey and I had decided to be together, I saw fewer and fewer angels out in the open. It was also harder for me to hear Evey from another room. I was losing my ability to protect her. I wondered if humans always felt that way... worried about the unknown, and constantly worried that something might happen to their loved ones. Maybe another angel was watching over Evey, and I just couldn't see him.

"Hello, earth to Lucian? Don't you agree that we need more space from each other?"

I looked over at Evey, glaring at me from the passenger seat, waiting for my response.

"If I knew for sure that another angel was assigned to you, I would say okay. I want us to be normal too, but I can't lose you. And I definitely can't lose you because I made the selfish decision to be with you."

"We're in love." She squeezed my hand but stayed looking straight ahead. "We're in love and we *are* normal, and we're going to have a baby." She took her phone from her purse and began dialing.

"Who are you calling?" I asked.

"Everyone. I'm telling everyone we're going to have a baby."

I grabbed the phone from her hand. "No!"

I felt her getting angry. "What is your problem? Your erratic behavior is starting to annoy me, Lucian."

"Oh God, we're fighting. We're having our first fight as a married couple." I was circling our block, looking for a parking space.

"This is normal conversation. You've been around long enough to know that. I can't believe how crazy you're acting."

"Me? I'm not acting crazy, you are. You're probably hormonal or something."

"Oh no you don't. Don't even go there. I resent that. Our baby probably resents that."

My hands were sweating on the steering wheel. I took a corner too fast, and the tires on Evey's shitty Honda squealed.

"Jesus, Lucian, are you trying to get us killed?"

"You need a new car!" I yelled. "This car is not safe!"

"This car is perfectly safe. You are the one who is not safe. You need to calm down."

I took a deep breath in through my nose. "I am calm Evey, but you're newfound need to be away from me is really pissing me off."

"You're pissed? I saw you checking out that blond nurse."

"What? Oh my God, now you're really being insane. I'm not attracted to women, for the millionth time."

"You're not attracted to women?"

"Other women, I mean."

"Oh, okay, and you expect me to believe that?" she snapped.

"You don't understand anything."

"Well, help me understand."

"I can't. I've tried. You're just special. You're different." I knew if I said soul mate, she'd laugh.

"I'm special? That nurse had a perfect body, and I saw you checking out her ass. Meanwhile, I can feel myself getting fatter by the minute."

I stopped arguing with her. I think *it was* the hormones.

I finally found a spot, parked, jumped out, and rushed to the passenger door with my hand out.

Evey pushed me away. "I can walk on my own. I have two legs still, last time I checked."

Once inside the apartment, she rushed off to our bedroom and slammed the door. I went to the living room and plopped onto the couch. I was fuming too. This wasn't going as planned. It got even worse when I heard Evey say under her breath, "God, he's annoying sometimes."

"I can hear you!" I yelled.

"Then turn off your angel ears, jerk!"

That was it. I marched down the hall and knocked on the door. "Can I come in?"

"Why even ask? Why don't you just beam yourself in here? You could be in here right now for all I know."

I turned the knob slowly and opened the door. Walking toward Evey as she lay on the bed, I noticed her eyes were closed, her arms crossed, and she was breathing heavily through her nose. She was very mad. Sitting on the edge of the bed, I took her hand. She resisted at first, but then finally gave in. She kept her eyes shut.

"First, no name-calling, and second, come here. I want to hold you, and I won't take no for an answer."

"I don't want to fight with you," she said with her eyes still closed.

"I don't want to fight either."

She finally looked at me, a little reluctantly at first, but it didn't take long for Evey's genuine kindness to come through. She crawled onto my lap, wrapping her legs around my body. I held her head to my chest.

"I'm as scared as you are," I said. She sniffled. "Please don't cry. I want to tell you that everything will be okay, but I just don't know anymore. I can't give you that comfort, and I feel terrible because of it." She kissed my neck while I tried to soothe her. "I'm going to leave you alone for a while. I'm going to try to do that more and trust that you'll be okay, that you'll watch out for yourself." She nodded into my shoulder. "Take a nap, my love. I'll be back in a few hours. Text me if you need anything."

We had exchanged numbers a week before our wedding, which we both found hysterical. Evey thought it was so funny to text me from the other room. I guess we were becoming sort of normal. I knew I had to get a job and find a way to still protect Evey but also be a person, a member of society... her husband.

I found a billboard off the 1 freeway to sit on and watch the traffic. I sat there for two hours, tempted to text Evey and see how she was doing, but I stayed strong. I blinked once, and Zack was sitting next to me. He looked back at the billboard. "Very apropos, man," he said. It was a photo of some shiny-haired dude next to the words *Jesus is watching you.* "Why do humans think Jesus was a white surfer from Southern California?"

I shrugged. "That's not even the best part. Look behind you." I directed Zack's attention to the XXX porn shop that sat just to the right of the billboard.

"It's intentional... the billboard?"

"Yeah." I laughed through my nose. "Humans are always so willing to judge, but they know nothing."

"Neither do we," he said.

"Exactly, so what's the point of the fake Jesus billboard? It says Jesus is watching, but pseudo-Jesus is smiling. I guess he's happy that you're in the porn shop?" Zack laughed and held his hand to his stomach. I was so happy to see him, and I knew he was happy to be there. I ruffled his hair. "I thought you weren't allowed to talk to me anymore?"

He shrugged and pointed at the billboard. "I'm sure he has bigger fish to fry, and anyway, Mona's been really cool."

"Didn't they assign Mona to another group?"

"Nah, they let her keep me. My good behavior, I guess. She was in hot water for a while, but that blew over. I also got my couple back, so I've been watching you and Evey from across the street. I followed you here. Why'd you take a cab, Lucian? And why aren't you with her, man? You guys fighting already?"

My hair was getting long. I tucked a strand behind my ear and thought idly that it was strange that my hair was growing. I had been exactly the same for two thousand years. "Now that Evey and I are married, I'm trying to make things seem more normal for her."

"But it's not ever going to be normal because of what she knows and what you are."

"It has to be though. We have to figure out a way. All we're doing is loving each other. There can't be anything wrong with that. We should get an award for that. How can it be wrong?"

"Big guy works in mysterious ways."

I sighed. "I wish people would stop saying that."

"Lucian, I know it's getting under your skin—all of those self-righteous angels who scoff at the two you as you walk down the street holding hands. Fuck them. You're in love with Evey, and that's all that matters."

"She's pregnant," I said.

He jerked his head back. "Whoa, whoa, whoa, pregnant? Wow. Pregnant?"

"Yes. The doctor confirmed it."

He was quiet for a minute. "What if it's like an alien baby?"

"You know there's no such thing as aliens, but thanks for the heartfelt congratulations, friend."

"How is it even possible? I've never heard of that."

"Maybe I'm becoming human," I said, hoping he'd agree.

"I don't know. So you don't know how it happened?"

"No clue, except, you know, we did it." I looked over at him and opened my eyes wide

"Yeah, I knew that part; I'm not that inexperienced. But just how is she pregnant?"

"No clue. Maybe I should ask Mona."

"She won't know. She knows nothing, except for when it's time to order coffee filters or who should get fucking cupcakes for their hard work. I asked her about my paycheck last week, and she said that accounting was on vacation, and she'd have to get back to me. Isn't that like their fifth vacation this year? I swear, it's a bureaucratic mess up there. Mona says she gets the runaround about everything. Every time she calls her supervisor, his secretary says he's in a meeting. You're not the only one being ignored."

"I know. It's like they sit in meetings all day and nothing ever gets done because all they do is talk, talk, talk. And then half the higher-ups leave the meeting and go on vacation. Not to mention summer Fridays. What the fuck is that? It's like high school up there. Did you know they actually take Fridays off during the summer? We don't have Fridays off, and we're doing all the work."

"I know, man. Mona has totally given up. That's why she hasn't been on your ass lately. She doesn't even know what's going on."

"I thought they'd at least want you to stop talking to me?"

He said something, but I couldn't hear him anymore. Then his image started to fade as he sat beside me.

"What are you doing?" I said.

"Nothing," he mouthed.

"I can't hear you."

"Can you hear me now?" He was clear again.

"Yeah, Jesus, that was weird. It's like I lost your signal."

"Fucking Verizon," he said jokingly.

"It's not funny. Weird things are happening to me."

"Welcome the change, Lucian. Honestly, weren't you bored out of your mind before anyway?"

"Weren't you?" I asked.

"No, I'm content. I like my life. I like what I do. Hey, I gotta go though." He looked at his watch. "*Top Chef* is almost over."

"Cool, man, good seeing you," I said.

He waved, then he was gone.

"Mona!" I yelled, but she never came.

I had an idea for how I would spend the rest of the day. First I texted Evey:

Me: *Everything okay?*

Evey: *I'm good. Just reading about pregnancy. Our baby is the size of a lentil.*

Me: *Wow, weird. I hope you don't give birth to a giant legume. You never know with us. It could be anything.*

Evey: *Stop, Lucian. What are you up to?*

Me: *Nothing much. Just hanging out. Might go see a movie or go jogging.*

Evey: *You swear to me you're not hovering in the corner?*

It occurred to me that for Evey, this was all kind of creepy.

Me: *I promise you, Evey. I'm going to take a walk right now. I'm far away and anyway, I won't ever watch you without telling you. Just please be safe.*

Evey: *I'm just lying here. Doors are locked. See you when you get home.*

Me: *Love you.*

Evey: *Love you too.*

Most normal conversation we had ever had. It was time for my experiment to begin. I stood, and a giant seagull dropped a load of shit on my shoulder. If that wasn't enough proof that I was becoming a human, I didn't know what was.

I flew poorly to the bay and dove in. Fuck, it was cold. I tried to hold my breath. I counted to three hundred then almost passed out, so I shot out of the water. I had a hard time getting lift with sopping wet, sparse wings and boots on. I found an empty public bathroom and dried my clothes under the hand dryer. Everything in me had weakened.

Next stop, the bridge. I went to the Golden Gate and stood on the railing for a long time, looking for angels. I couldn't see any. I started teetering like I was going to fall. I was visible to humans.

I heard someone gasp and a woman scream, "He's going to jump!"

Then there was a voice behind me. "You don't want to do that, man."

I turned around and saw the faint outline of wings.

"You're an angel," I said to the man, but why didn't he know I was? It just validated my point even further. He couldn't see my wings. I jumped down and stood face to face with him.

"I'm not an angel, but if I've convinced you not to jump, then I'm very happy to know that." He was lying. Those lies we tell.

I leaned in and whispered, "I can see your wings, man." I extended mine to their full glory.

"Oh, I didn't see yours before. Let's get out of here before we make a scene," he said. "Nothin' to see here, people." He tugged on my shoulder, pulling me down the walkway. "Once we get to the end, cloak yourself and meet me on Pier 39."

"I hate that place. Too crowded."

"My souls are down there. I've got to get back. Just saw your little stunt and flew over here."

I followed him to Pier 39, although it was hard to keep up with him. We stayed cloaked and found an empty bench to occupy.

"So what's your name?" I said.

"Leo." He looked like a newer version but not as new as Zack.

"I'm Lucian." I shook his hand.

"Oh, Lucian. I heard about you."

"What'd you hear?"

"You the one who married one of your souls."

"Word spreads fast," I said.

"Yeah, I was banging this chick, Abigail—"

"Yeah, I know her." Fucking Abigail, such a big-mouthed brat.

"Sweet little ass, huh?" Leo said. I just shrugged like I had no idea what he was talking about. "So what were you doing on the bridge?"

I was texting Evey and mindlessly responding to Leo at the same time. "Just trying something out."

Me: *You ok?*

Evey: *Yes fine, have fun.*

"Trying something out?" Leo said.

"Well, I have this theory. Since I've been with my soul, my angel gifts, so to speak, have been failing or fading. I don't know, just changing."

"So what's your theory?"

"That I'm becoming a human." I looked at him and arched my eyebrows.

He shook his head. "Nah, no way. It can't happen."

"Really, you don't think it's possible?"

"No."

"Evey, my wife, is pregnant."

"With what?"

"See, that's my point," I said. "It's not a litter of fucking puppies, man. She's pregnant with my baby."

"I don't know."

"It's true."

He looked off into a restaurant, seeming to think about what I had said. "Hey, let me get these two home. Then you wanna grab a drink, and we'll talk some more?"

I looked into the restaurant and saw a couple enjoying a meal. "Are those your souls right there?"

"Yeah."

"Looks like they're enjoying themselves."

"Give me a second." He opened his hand and revealed a giant roach.

"No, you can't do that."

He shook his head. "Yeah, I can. These two never stay home. I'm constantly following their asses around the city. I could use a beer."

He left me on the bench, then a moment later he was following two very angry people out of the restaurant. Leo was laughing and waving for me to follow. I would never have done that to one of my souls.

WE ENDED UP at the Star Wars bar, and Han, the bartender working when Evey first met me, was manning the bar once again.

"You," he said when we sat down. "I thought you'd be dead." He addressed Leo, "Your friend can drink."

"Whiskeys and IPAs," Leo said.

Han poured us two fingers of Whistle Pig and some local IPAs in pints. Leo dumped part of his IPA beer into his whiskey, so I did the same. I'd told Evey that I wouldn't drink like that, but we were fighting, and I needed something. I downed the first cup then the second, and I was toast. My body wasn't recovering very fast.

Leo was looking at me strangely. "Why are you so fucked up, man?"

"I don't know. This is what's happening to me." I shook my head. "I can only have one more, then I gotta get home."

"Home?" he repeated. It wasn't exactly angel-speak.

"Yeah, I gotta get home to Evey. She's pregnant, and she's gonna get mad at me for getting trashed."

"The old ball and chain, huh? Been married a few days and you're already fighting and in trouble?"

"No, it's not like that," I said, but it kind of was. "I just wanted to know if you had ever heard of anything like this happening?"

"What?" Leo said.

"Angels falling for their souls and what happens to them. Can they have babies?"

He laughed. "Fallen angel, what a cliché."

"Yeah, I know. Just tell me though."

"No, I've never heard of anything like that."

"I got to go." I threw some cash on the bar and waved to Han.

He smiled and waved back.

"Bye," Leo called but didn't turn around. "Good luck with all that cosmic shit you're fucking with."

"Asshole," I said under my breath.

I texted Evey.

Me: *B home n 5*

Evey: *Can you get me some Cherry Garcia?*

Ice cream cravings already? That was a good sign.

Me: *Of course!*

When I came in holding a pint of Evey's favorite ice cream, she was smiling and as happy as ever. "There's my prince," she said.

"I have a feeling that anyone holding a pint of Cherry Garcia would be your prince."

"Not true," she sang. "Have you been drinking?"

"Yes, but I know my limit now."

"Good." She kissed my nose while she took the ice cream from my hand.

"Can I lick this off of you?" I asked.

"Best idea you've had, husband."

Things finally felt right again. I was licking ice cream off of Evey's thighs, and heaven was here on Earth. I was sure of that.

15

HOLY WAR

Evelyn

I COULDN'T BELIEVE that Lucian was searching Want Ads for a job. He was lying next to me in our bed, circling ads and laughing at how overqualified he was.

"This one says, 'Must be bilingual.' Should I put on my résumé that I speak seventeen languages?"

"Don't be arrogant. People don't like arrogant."

He rolled over and kissed my tummy. "Hello, baby." He looked up at me. "Should we find out if it's a boy or a girl?"

"We can find out at the next ultrasound." So far, everything was coming along perfectly. We were pregnant with an actual baby, as far as the doctor could tell.

He yawned. "Are you tired?"

"Yeah, but not that tired. It's only seven," I said.

"Mm, I can't wait to meet you," he said to my stomach.

I was eleven weeks pregnant. We were a family. Lucian and I had fights, but we were a family, and we were working things out and figuring out how to be normal.

"You have an interview tomorrow, don't you? At that financial firm?"

"Yeah. I'm going to drive you to work, then I'll pick you up," he said.

"Okay."

In the morning, we got up like it was any other day. Lucian made my favorite breakfast—avocado on toast with olive oil and tomato. I smiled when I took it from him. "You're too good to me."

"It's only because you're carrying my baby," he said with a smirk.

"By the way, I meant to ask you. Does our little one have an angel hanging around?"

He squinted and shook his head slowly. "No, it's just you and me until she's born."

"She? You know?"

"No, no, just have a feeling. Wishful thinking, I guess."

"You want a girl then?"

"I'd be happy either way, but yeah, I was just thinking how beautiful and kind-hearted she'd be... like her mom."

We drove across the bridge as Lucian sang along to Leon Bridges. "You have a good voice," I told him.

"So do you."

"You've never heard me sing."

"Evey, I've heard you sing a million times."

I blushed. That's right—he'd heard everything. "That's not fair."

"Sing with me."

I tried to sing along but couldn't hold a candle to Lucian's singing. He said he'd been doing it longer, which was a silly understatement. He dropped me at Tracey's warehouse, and then headed off for his job interview.

As he was pulling away, he stopped the car, rolled down the window, and said, "Check your messenger bag. I made you lunch so you don't have to leave. Please don't leave here without me. Text me if anything comes up."

"Don't worry about me. Good luck." I kissed him once more through the open window.

I spent the morning doing sketches for Tracey, and by lunch, I was starving and feeling woozy. I hadn't texted Lucian because I didn't want to distract him, but I was feeling mildly crampy. By two o'clock, the cramps were getting worse. I called Dr. Smythe.

"You should come in, Evelyn, so we can do an ultrasound and check you out. If it gets worse, go to the ER."

As soon as I pressed End on the phone, I texted Lucian.

Me: *I'm feeling crampy. Gonna ask Tracey to drive me to the doctor's.*

Lucian: *No, I'll be there in two minutes.*

Tracey was in the back room as I stood at the front window waiting. I felt a gush of fluid between my legs and a sharp, shooting pain. I dropped to my knees on the hard concrete. Blood seeped through my jeans. I heard a thud as Lucian landed hard just outside of the door. He had flown there.

"What was that?" Tracey said as she came walking out from the back room.

Lucian completely ignored her. He was laser-focused on me. He stalked over to me and lifted me with ease. His wings were spread and flapping.

"No," he whimpered. "No."

"How are we going to get there?" I asked.

"Oh my God," Tracey said, falling to the floor when she saw Lucian.

Lucian finally realized she was standing there, witnessing the entire thing. He set me down gently. "One second." He marched with resolute concentration toward a terrified Tracey.

"No," she said, holding up her hand in an attempt to block Lucian from whatever he was about to do.

He pressed a thumb to her forehead. Her eyes rolled back in her head. "Stop, Lucian, you're hurting her." He didn't even seem to hear me. Tracey was writhing on the floor. The smell of burning skin wafted toward me, as Lucian pressed his thumb to her forehead even harder.

"Stop, Lucian," I screamed.

He pulled away, turned to the empty space next to him, and spoke to someone I couldn't see. "I had to. I'm sorry. She'll be fine."

Tracey was still unconscious.

"What's going on?" I started to cry.

Lucian was at my side in a millisecond, and I was in his arms again. "She'll be okay. I couldn't let her say anything. We have to go."

A moment later, we were in the air, flying fast. We landed hard on the roof of San Francisco General Hospital. Lucian was undeterred and mysterious again. My angel, trying to protect me. I couldn't see my husband in him anymore.

He didn't speak as he carried me to the roof door and kicked it open with little effort. In the elevator, he scanned my body.

"It's over," I told him. "She's gone."

"No." There was no expression in his eyes. He managed to carry me into triage without even checking in and yelled, "My wife needs help quickly."

A nurse was at my side in a moment. There was blood all over my pants, but the pain had stopped. Lucian slumped into a chair in the corner, rested his elbows on his spread knees, and dropped his face into his hands. I couldn't tell if he was crying, but he was obviously in pain.

"It's okay, Lucian," I whispered.

"You've lost a lot of blood," the nurse said.

There was a blur of doctors and nurses. I heard the words miscarriage, hemorrhaging, and hematoma. My clothes were removed. I was cleaned and then moved to another room. I was woozy, but Lucian was next to me, still inscrutable.

"What's happening?" When I tried to sit up, I lost consciousness.

Moments later, I came to and heard Lucian yelling something, but I couldn't make out what he was saying. I closed my eyes and wanted to disappear. I had lost the baby.

Then I was in an operating room, and a doctor I didn't know was telling me that he was going to perform a procedure to remove the fetus, placenta, and hematoma. Lucian was holding my hand. They sedated me.

I didn't remember anything after that until I woke up in a

recovery room. When I opened my eyes, I saw Lucian sitting in a chair in the corner. All of the lights were off, and the curtains were drawn. I couldn't see his face well enough to read his expression. "I've gone too far," he said in a low voice. "I can't fix this. I can't erase your memory. I can't erase the memories of everyone I've met because of you. I only have one choice now, Evey."

"Don't you dare." I knew what he meant. "You do not get to leave me, Lucian."

"I can't see you like this, knowing that I did this to you."

"You did not do this to me. I had a miscarriage. Women have them all the time."

"You don't care? You don't care that we lost our little girl?"

I started to cry. "Was it a girl?"

He nodded in the darkness. I cried full, quiet sobs, but Lucian didn't come to comfort me. Instead, he left the room. I rolled onto my side and cried even harder.

"Please come back to me," I said, but he didn't. "Don't do this to me."

I knew he could hear me. He couldn't have gotten far.

The doctor came in and said he wanted to keep me overnight. I said, "Okay," and then dozed off alone. I woke sometime after midnight. It was completely dark, but I could see that Lucian was back, in the same chair again. I smelled whiskey. I closed my eyes and feigned sleep, but a moment later, he was standing over me; I could feel him.

"Why? Why, God?" He was in pain. Tormented Lucian would not be easy to talk to. My eyes were closed when I felt his lips on my forehead. "Good-bye, Evey. I love you."

Without opening my eyes, I said, "Whatever you're

thinking about doing, forget it. It's not happening." I looked up at him.

His face was swollen and red with tears. "I can't put you through any more hell than I already have."

"I had a miscarriage. It had nothing to do with you." I started to cry. "What are you going to do? Kill yourself? You're going to leave me after we've been married and I'm lying in a hospital bed because I've had a miscarriage? How could you do that to me?"

He shook his head and smiled, small and tight. "You won't remember anything," he said softly. He looked pleased with himself.

"I *want* to remember *everything*."

"Not this."

"Lucian, please."

The nurse came in and pushed more pain medication through my IV.

"Please, Lucian, don't do anything stupid." As I started to doze off from the pain medicine, I chanted the prayer out loud. The nurse was gone. It was just the two of us.

He held his hand to my forehead and said it with me. "Angel of God, my Guardian dear to whom His love commits me here, ever this night be at my side, to light and guard, to rule and guide. Amen."

Everything was black after that.

16

POOF

Lucian

SHE WOULDN'T REMEMBER a thing, and no one else would either. I'd be gone and leave no mark at all. Poof, just like that. She'd be free of me. Someone would be assigned to protect her, she'd meet a real man, and everything would be fine. She'd have babies and healthy pregnancies and a good life and a great career. I'd gotten her this far; I couldn't ruin her now.

It felt like days that I was standing there, on the edge of the highway. All it would take was walking five feet. I saw a bus coming and timed it. Five... four... three... then my phone buzzed.

Evey: *I need you now. Please, I'm hurting.*

Every time I thought about Evey in pain, it felt as though I was being burned at the stake. Was this His divine comedy?

Flying back to the hospital, I fell to the ground three times. I could barely fly anymore.

When I entered her hospital room, she was shaking her head at me. "Some husband you are. Running off to kill yourself while your wife sobs in a hospital room alone."

"You don't understand, Evelyn."

"Neither do you," she yelled.

There was a nurse on the other side of the room, restocking the cabinets.

"Take it easy."

"I know what you were gonna do. Are you insane? The doctor said that had I not had that hematoma, the baby and pregnancy would have probably been normal." She jabbed a finger at my chest.

"Ow, easy."

"Come closer, you jerk." Evey grabbed my ear and yanked me toward her face.

"Geez, relax. I fell hard three times on my way over here. I'm kind of sore."

"Bet getting your ear tugged on is nothing compared to being hit by a bus," she whispered. I started to pull away, but she yanked me back down. "Did you hear anything? They said the fetus was otherwise healthy." Her voice was getting louder. "No wings detected. Just normal human baby parts, Lucian, you ass."

I shook my head. "Shh. No need for name-calling, Evey. Anyway, I still don't think it's possible."

"Will you just wait and see? What if you really are

becoming human?" She glanced at the clock. "I'm tired. It's four in the morning."

It was getting close to magic hour. I could have gone out and gotten drunk or tried to find answers, but instead, I crawled into bed next to Evey and rested my head on her chest. I put my hand on her belly, and she laced her fingers through mine. We cried together and then fell asleep. Our baby was gone.

THINGS CHANGED OVER the next few weeks. I insisted on using condoms, but soon gave up on that. It's just not the same. Tracey gave me a job working in the warehouse, which allowed me to stay close to Evey, but it also irritated her. She wanted independence. I understood, even though she often forgot that I had always been there. She'd tell me it was just different now.

On a Tuesday, Brooklyn came down to the warehouse and flaunted a giant diamond. Evey just stared at it in shock.

"Congrats," I said from behind Brooklyn. "Who's the lucky guy?" *Poor fool.*

"Oh my God, you work here now too?" Brooklyn said. "You guys really can't be away from each other for more than a minute."

She had no idea. Evey didn't respond, and I didn't want to explain.

"So who is he?" I asked again.

"Keith," Evey answered for Brooklyn.

I pointed at Evey, "Keith, as in the Keith you went out with?"

"Yes. Although he wasn't really himself that night, so I didn't get to know him at all." Evey rolled her eyes at me.

"You're marrying that guy?" I said.

"Lucian," Evey chided.

"What's it to you, weirdo?" Brooklyn asked.

"Nothing," I said. "Congrats, weirdo." I was done being a jerk to Brooke. She didn't deserve it.

I turned and walked away, but I could still hear Evey talking. They started planning Brooklyn's wedding right then and there. Brooklyn had gone from not wanting to go on two dates with the same person to getting hitched. Maybe Evey had more of an influence on her than I had thought.

While the two girls were talking wedding details, I went to the back of the warehouse to break down boxes. I noticed a huge pile of jeans in a tote sitting next to the dumpster. They were Evey's designs.

I grabbed the jeans, went inside, and marched up to Tracey. "You're throwing these out?"

"They're terrible," she said distractedly while she flipped through a magazine.

"I think they're great."

She set the magazine down and looked at me. "You think everything she does is great."

"That's not true. I hate when she whines. She also leaves the refrigerator open and the lights on." I actually didn't care about any of that. "But these are jeans are great, and you know it. She was willing to put your name on them. What, you have too much pride to let her designs take off? You know they will."

"They're just jeans," she said.

"Fine, then we'll take them. No sense in throwing out perfectly good denim."

"It's my denim, and if I want to throw it out, then I will."

"You're kidding, right?"

"No." She returned her focus to the magazine and flipped through the pages again.

"I've always been respectful toward you, Tracey—"

"I don't give a shit."

Tracey was truly a piece of work. I used to be able to charm women, but I didn't seem to have that effect on Tracey anymore. Actually, I didn't seem to have that effect on anyone anymore.

I set the jeans under a folding table and found Evey saying good-bye to Brooklyn outside.

Brooklyn smiled but held up her middle finger at me as she drove away.

"Can you be nice, Lucian?" Evey pleaded.

"I'm trying to be nice to Brooke. Tracey on the other hand, no, I can't be nice to her. Listen..." I held her shoulders. "Look at me. Look into my eyes."

She laughed. "What is up with you?"

"Do I look different?"

"What do you mean?"

"You know what I mean. Am I less attractive than when you met me?"

Her expression softened; she stopped laughing. "Aside from the fact that you're thinner and your hair is a little longer, you look exactly the same." She cupped my face. "You're ridiculously handsome, Lucian."

"You're the only one who thinks so."

"Are you being vain or insecure? It's hard to tell."

I kissed her slowly, softly. I felt her honesty in the kiss, and it didn't matter what anyone else thought of me.

She whispered, "You're learning to be human."

I whispered back, "Tracey is a bitch."

"We established that a long time ago...

I rested my head on her shoulder. "She tried to throw away your jeans."

Evey jerked her head back. "Really? Why?"

"I don't know. Jealous, I guess. Let's just take them. We'll get you a place and start your own brand."

"*Our* own brand," she said. "Eves is kind of already taken."

I laughed. "We'll think of a name."

"How about Divine?" .

"It's perfect." I kissed her nose. "Let's go tell Tracey off."

Evey walked into the warehouse and grabbed her sketchbook, the jeans, and a few other things. Nonchalantly, she said, "Lucian and I quit. This is my stuff, and I'm taking it. Good luck, Tracey."

Tracey didn't object, she just said, "Fine. I can find someone better. You can have the jeans. They're terrible anyway."

Evey smiled sincerely and said, "Good luck, Tracey."

Even in the worst situations, Evey had grace. I put my arm around her as we walked out. "You did good," I told her.

That marked the end of the Tracey era for Evey and me.

TWO MONTHS LATER, I was doing odd jobs to make money, losing more feathers here and there, and feeling less angelic by the day. Meanwhile, Evey carried on as though it wasn't unusual at all to be married to something that wasn't human. I didn't know what I was anymore.

We had saved enough money to float us for a few months until Evey could get her business off the ground. I had to assure her that I had taken the money from really bad people. She wasn't always convinced, and then I would just remind her that I personally knew Jesus Christ. We would both laugh because it just didn't seem like that was the reality anymore, even though I knew him in my heart still.

We were cleaning up a loft in the city, getting it ready to become Evey's workspace. It had taken us a while to find the perfect spot. The loft was a huge high-beamed space with concrete floors and floor-to-ceiling windows that spanned almost the entire side of one block.

"I think we should try to buy this place," she said while we swept dust into giant mounds. "The neighborhood is being overhauled. It'll probably be worth millions in a few years."

I started coughing and tried to clear my throat. I had to stop sweeping to catch my breath; the place was filthy. I felt like we were in over our heads, but she was happy. That was all that mattered. "Let's look into it."

"We can convert it to a live/work space," she said.

"That's a great idea. We'll work on it."

"With a nursery."

I stopped sweeping and looked up from the floor. Evey had stopped sweeping too. I scanned her from head to toe. She was wearing a timid smile, leaning on the broom.

"Evelyn," I said in a warning tone.

"You put a baby in me, Lucian."

"Jesus."

"No you," she said.

The ongoing joke was no longer funny. I was terrified inside, afraid that we'd have to endure the pain of loss all over again.

Stalking toward her, I dropped the broom with a thud, took her in my arms, and held her close. I could hear the baby's heart beating, like I'd had with Evey's last pregnancy. Although beautiful, I wished that the sound I was hearing was more reassuring. It would be for normal people. I buried my face in Evey's neck.

She held me tight and whispered, "Tell me you're happy."

My throat tightened. "I'm happy, Evey. Worried but happy."

"Please don't worry. Let's just take this one day at a time."

I nodded into her neck, but quickly pulled out of her embrace. It hit me, the possibility of it really happenening. I felt intense joy that overshadowed the fear. Real joy that Evey and I could become parents. "I have to go tell someone," I said excitedly. "How far along are you? How do you know? Why didn't you tell me?"

"I'm probably about seven weeks. I just wanted to wait until after I missed my period. I wanted to be sure. Brooklyn brought me a test when you were out one day."

"I'm going to be a father. I have to go tell someone." I was practically jumping out of my skin.

"You're so cute. Go, go tell someone. While you're out, you should look for a suit for Brooklyn's wedding. It's in three weeks."

"Right," I shouted as I headed for the elevator. I turned on my heel and ran back to Evey, took her in my arms, and spun her around. "I am so happy. I love you so much, but you should be wearing a mask or a ventilator here, okay? I'll bring you back one. No more sweeping." I set her down and headed back for the elevator.

"Get a suit, Lucian!"

Running out to the sidewalk, I cloaked myself and took flight, though not a steady flight with my now-very-depleted wings. I called for Zack or Mona and looked around for other angels but found no one I recognized. I really wanted to tell someone, and the only person I could think of was the bartender, Han. I headed for the Star Wars bar, and sure enough, he was working.

He pointed at me as I walked toward the bar. "Bullet neat?"

"Sure," I said a bit apprehensively. It was only eleven in the morning, but I wanted to celebrate. I sat on a red vinyl bar stool. "So, Han—"

"The name's Greg," he interrupted.

"Greg, I have some news."

"Oh, yeah?"

"Yeah." There was something unusually familiar about Greg.

He poured my drink and smiled in a knowing way. "What's happening to you?"

"What do you mean?"

He shook his head. "Never mind. So what's your news?"

I took a sip. "So, um, remember Evelyn? The girl that I walked home that one night? She used to come in here once in a while?"

"I remember," he said, laughing.

I didn't understand why he was acting so strange.

"She's pregnant. We're going to have a baby." I shot him an ear-splitting grin.

He didn't smile back. He refilled my drink and then leaned over the bar. "You don't have a clue, do you, Lucian?"

Had I ever told him my name? I didn't think so. "Clue about what?"

As he moved an inch closer to my face, I recognized something in his greenish eyes. "Who are you?" I asked.

"I got banished. I tried to sleep with Brooklyn, and Mona caught me."

"Zack?"

He rolled his eyes and nodded. "You're really losing it, man. Like, what is wrong with you?"

"Why do you look like this guy? And you were so good! How could she banish you?"

"I'm this guy forever. It's part of my punishment." I didn't want to tell him that his new look was actually an improvement. "It wasn't just the Brooklyn thing," he said. "They found out I was zapping my couple pretty bad so they would stay in the house and be a little confused."

"Wow! That really is pretty despicable, man."

"Yeah, I know. I feel bad," he said, but I wasn't sure he really did. "So I hate to break it to you, Lucian—because you're my friend—but you must know that things will eventually drop for you. Storm clouds are forming."

"Geez, Zack, why don't you be a little more cryptic? You're starting to sound like Mona now. And don't tell me bad things are going to happen if you have no clue at all." I looked around to see if anyone was in earshot of us. "Why do you want to ruin this for me? I think I'm becoming human. I think it's really happening."

"You're definitely losing your gifts, that's for sure. You should have spotted me in a second." He started wiping down the counter as he continued. "I don't know. But I can't be in this dude's body, in this shitty bar for an eternity while you're off living the life. Where's the justice in that?"

I stood and pushed the stool back forcefully, sending it screeching back a few feet. I threw a twenty on the counter. "Thanks for being a good friend. Sorry, you got thrown out. Don't blame me though, Zack. I had nothing to do with it."

When I turned to walk away, he said quietly, "Storm's coming."

"Fuck you," I said, without turning around. I was sad our friendship was coming to an end that way. Zack was just bitter.

I tried to fly home but couldn't get off the ground, so I started walking. I walked and walked, feeling more pathetic than ever. I wasn't a man or an angel. I was nothing. I popped into another bar and found a normal bartender to chat with. I drank three whiskeys, told him how excited I was about having a baby. I hoped he'd give me some congratulatory life hacks, but instead it was all negative.

"Listen brother, prepare thyself. You are so in for it," he said. "You should kiss sleeping good-bye right now." Not that sleepless nights would be a new thing for me, though I was needing more and more of it as time went on.

"Also, there won't be any time for this..." He gestured toward the glass. "Drinking in bars midday unless you want your wife to leave you. And one other thing—you're probably not gonna get any action for a while. They get what they want—a baby—and that's all we're needed for. She'll literally be repulsed by you."

"What? That can't be true." I had been made to make Evey feel good.

"You're just a man," he said. "There's only so much you can do."

I was feeling terrible and drunk. My superhero metabolism was no longer working at all. On the way back home, I passed a department store and popped in to get a suit. The woman helping me kept saying, "Are you sure you want all black? Black shirt, tie, everything?"

"Yes."

"Do you need some dress shoes?"

"Something wrong with these boots?" I said.

"Let me help you. You're too damn good-looking to spoil your suit with shoes like that. Let's get you a white shirt and some nice shoes and keep everything else black, okay?"

"Sure," I slurred. My ears perked up at her compliment. *Good-looking.*

She brushed my dick accidentally while she was measuring my inseam. "Oh, sorry about that," she said, blushing.

"It's okay, baby." *Oh no, the Lucian evolution. Lucian: the angel, the drunk, the mortal pervert.*

She glanced at my wedding ring. "What's the occasion?"

"Friend's wedding," I said.

She was an attractive woman, but I wasn't attracted to her. I was just getting the attention I hadn't gotten from Evey in a while. Evey had been swept up in Brooklyn's wedding and the new studio loft, and now she would be swept up in a baby and have no time for me. I wondered if it was all worth it. I was changing fast. When I went to step into the dressing room, the woman hesitated outside it. She stared at me and glanced past me into the empty dressing room space. It was a come on. *I've still got it.* But I shook my head at her.

She looked away and said, "I'll be out here when you're dressed."

Evey had texted me to meet her back at the apartment since I was taking forever, according to her. I believe her texts were starting to get naggy, but that might have been me being sensitive.

When I walked through the door, she yelled from the couch, "Finally!" Her tone was not pleasant.

I slurred, "Honey, I'm home."

"I'm not laughing, Lucian. Where were you?"

I walked up to her and held out a receipt. "I got a suit. It'll be ready in a couple of days."

She was sitting on the couch with her legs and arms crossed. There was no expression on her face. "Did it take five hours?"

"I ran into Zack."

"Do I smell whiskey?"

"Evey, there is no way you can smell my breath from down there."

"I'm pregnant, Lucian." She tossed a copy of *What to Expect When You're Expecting* in my direction. "My sense of smell is heightened."

"Oh. Well, I had a couple of drinks." I looked at my feet, ashamed.

She huffed as she stood from the couch. "I'm showering," she said, walking past me.

"I'll join you."

"That's okay."

It's happening. I followed her down the hall and went past the bathroom to our bedroom. When I heard the water go on, I decided I wasn't going to sit back and let that bartender be right. We needed make-up sex. I stalked into the bathroom and stripped down.

I opened the shower curtain. At first she scowled, then her expression softened.

"I want to touch my wife." I waited for her to give me permission.

She nodded infinitesimally. That was enough. Pressing myself against her back, I felt her relax. I kissed her neck, and she moaned.

"I do need this, Lucian," she said.

"I know."

I moved my hand lower and touched her until she was writhing in my arms. I turned her around and slammed my mouth into hers. She bit my lip hard.

I pulled back. "Ow. You taking your frustrations out on me?"

"No, I just want it rough. You've been too easy on me, too gentle. I want strong Lucian back."

I picked her up to straddle me and pressed her hard against the tile. "I'm worried about the baby."

"It'll be okay. Just fuck me."

Whoa. That pretty much did me in. I was moving hard inside her.

"You're the only one who can do this to me," she said.

"Well, I hope so."

She was falling apart in my arms... trembling. "Oh,

Lucian, don't baby me."

"Don't say the word baby right now." I moved harder and harder, and she was sopping wet everywhere.

That bartender was full of shit. Evey was into it.

Later that night, as we lay in bed, we talked about our plans. Evey kept saying, "One step at a time." But I had the vague sense that I needed to speed things up.

17

TWO STEPS FORWARD

Evelyn

IT WAS VINTAGE Lucian in the shower that night... strong, powerful, sexy Lucian. Something had come over him. He fell asleep first, which was unusual, but then again, he had hit the whiskey and then expended quite a bit of energy on me.

Halfway through the night, he woke me up when he made a pained sound. He started coughing, so I mindlessly rubbed his back and reached for some water. I was mortified at what happened next. I felt bone and feather breaking apart, disintegrating in my hand. Lucian was weak. He began moaning, so I felt his forehead; he was burning up.

"Lucian," I whispered.

"I don't feel well, Evey."

"Your wings. Try to sit up."

He sat up while I flipped on the light. He was wearing only boxer briefs, so I could see his back. I saw nothing—no wings, feathers, blood, or broken pieces. He had his elbows resting on his knees over the edge of the bed with his head drooping into his hands.

"Everything hurts," he said.

"Show me your wings, Lucian."

"I'm not hiding anything from you."

They were gone. I felt his back frantically. He fell back into my arms. I held him in my lap. "They're gone, Lucian."

"I know," he said.

"I'm going to CVS to get you some medicine. You have a fever. You might have the flu."

"I shouldn't be near you and the baby."

I ignored him and got up to get dressed. "Lie down. I'll bring you more water."

He fell back onto the pillow. After I brought him water, I kissed his forehead and headed out. It was the second time I'd ever left the safety of our home or the loft without Lucian. The first time was just the day before.

Things were changing.

When I returned from the pharmacy, he was curled in a ball, shaking. He could barely speak. His teeth were chattering. "Evey, you can't go out like that without me."

"I'm fine. I'll be fine."

I gave him Tylenol and wrapped him in blankets. Over the next four hours, I stroked his hair and wiped sweat from his forehead. He would doze off then startle awake.

"What's happening, Lucian?"

"I don't know. I know nothing."

"I'm taking you to the hospital." I stood abruptly and felt a gush between my legs. *No.* I held my hand between my legs. "No."

Lucian looked up at me. "What? What is it?"

Scrambling to the bathroom, I felt the familiar cramping. "No!"

Lucian was behind me, looking pale and weak. I closed the bathroom door as he waited in the hallway. "Tell me what's going on. Is it happening again?"

Sitting on the toilet, I felt all of the hope, all of the promise leave my body in less than a minute. I cried loudly and dropped my head to my knees. I felt defeated. "God, why are you taking all of this away from us?"

The next thing I knew, Lucian was there with me in the bathroom. He had come through the door somehow, just like he used to. He had cloaked himself, but I felt his familiar comfort around my shoulders.

"I know you're here," I said. "You can show yourself."

The feeling became even stronger, and then I heard his voice. It was almost as if he was far away. He said, "This is all I have left. This is all I can give you."

I cleaned myself up as best as I could and stood. When I opened the door, Lucian was standing there. I collapsed into his arms.

"This is too much, isn't it?" he said.

"Don't give up, please. Don't give up on us." I pressed my hand to his head. He was still burning up. Was he burning up literally? "We both need to go to the hospital."

He cupped my face. "Look at me, Evey." I looked into his glistening blue eyes and saw all of his love in them. "You are everything to me. You're the dream, the air, the reason, the cause for my whole existence. If I die today right in front of you, it won't be because I gave up. I'll never give up. There is no God that can keep me from you. I'd die ten thousand times for you. I've been this *thing*, this being that no one believed in. I had no legacy. I had to be selfless for so long, then I found you and you always gave more than you took. When you were little, I used to think everything you did was amazing... I still do. I've loved you forever. You don't understand that my life before you was nothing. You made me real. You made me exist... finally. I would take this pain all over again. I wouldn't change anything."

I felt tears streaming steadily down my cheeks. Listening to every word that came out of his beautiful mouth, I wondered what I would be without him. If I lost him, I would die. "Don't say things like that. We're going to be okay," I told him.

He smiled, but there was still so much sadness in his eyes. Wiping the tears from my cheek with his thumb, he bent and kissed my lips. "Always the optimist."

I was trembling from the cramps. Lucian, as weak as he was, picked me up, grabbed the keys, and carried me out to the car. When we reached the hospital, he yelled for someone to help me. I shuffled to a wheelchair just outside of the ER doors, then a nurse wheeled me in, asking me questions.

"I'm having a miscarriage, and my husband is very sick. He should be coming in behind me." I heard a ruckus from the entrance and saw staff running toward the doors.

The nurse stopped pushing me and glanced back.

"What's happening?" I asked.

The nurse didn't answer. She just stared, eyes wide. I stood on shaking legs and looked back at the entrance. Just

214

inside the doorway, Lucian was on the floor, convulsing. I ran to him, feeling blood running down my legs. My gray sweats were drenched.

"Ma'am," one of the nurses said, but I ignored her.

A doctor was trying to prevent Lucian from banging his head on the ground. His eyes had rolled back in his head, and he was foaming at the mouth.

I was crying and screaming, "Help him!"

"Whose blood is that?" one nurse said.

Then I heard, "It's the woman who's bleeding."

"Help my husband," I screamed through what felt like an hour of watching Lucian convulse. "Please, help him!"

"We're doing what we can," a blond woman in blue scrubs said to me as we all sat on the floor around him.

When the seizure started to subside, Lucian was still twitching. His eyes were back, but he was obviously confused.

"Ma'am, you need help. Let us help you," the lady in scrubs said to me.

I need help?

Lucian tried to focus his eyes and sit up, but the staff wouldn't let him. Four men lifted him onto a gurney. When I stood, Lucian glanced at my sweats and began crying. He was trying to form words, but everyone was telling him to relax and take it easy. He reached his hand out to me and I felt it, the energy he was giving me.

When he started to close his eyes, one of the nurses said, "Try to stay awake, sir."

He was losing consciousness by trying to give me strength.

"His name is Lucian," I said as I followed the gurney out

of the ER lobby.

I was still holding his hand, hoping I could give him some comfort. He was fighting it, I could tell, trying to keep his eyes open. He seemed so human, but I knew he wasn't. I wondered what kind of tests they would run on him and if they would somehow be able to tell that he was something other than a man.

The nurse who had been pushing me in the wheelchair earlier was urging me to sit back down. I let go of Lucian's hand, and his eyes shot open.

"I'm sorry," he mouthed.

I collapsed into the chair, and then Lucian and I were wheeled in different directions. I had to have a vaginal ultrasound to confirm that my baby no longer had a heartbeat. My baby was dead and gone... again. I felt naked inside and out, vulnerable, alone, sick to my stomach, depressed. I missed Lucian and couldn't stop thinking about how he must have been feeling. I yearned for him to be there with me.

Probing my bleeding insides, the man watched a screen and said without any compassion, "There's nothing in there."

"Excuse me?"

He glanced at my face quickly before looking back at the screen. Pointing at something, he said, "That's your uterus, and there's nothing in there."

I wondered whether I should thank him or punch him. It was like déjà vu, being in that situation, in pain and not knowing how to act, whether to be angry or sad. They wheeled me into another room to recover, except this time I was alone. The nurse asked if I wanted pain medication, and I told her no. A male doctor I had never met came in and said that I had miscarried and that everything was fine. But it wasn't. What a poor choice of words. I had just miscarried. Everything wasn't fine.

"What's wrong with me?" I asked.

He squinted, looking confused.

When he opened his mouth to speak, I interrupted him. "This is my second miscarriage. Why is this happening?"

He cleared his throat. "We contacted your OBGYN, so you'll want to follow up with her, but miscarriages are very common. Consider it your body's way of ridding what would likely be an unviable fetus."

Unviable fetus? Again, poor choice of words. "But it already had a heartbeat."

He approached the head of the bed. He put his cold hand on my arm. "I'm very sorry this happened to you. Try to look at it as a blessing."

"A blessing?" He nodded, and I shook my head. "Will you please give me an update on my husband, Lucian Casey?"

"Sure. I'll be right back."

No one returned. A half an hour later, I was buzzing the nurses station like a lunatic. Yet another nurse I had never seen before, wearing Pepto-colored scrubs, came skipping in, her ponytail swinging from left to right as if her hair itself was happy being attached to her head. I wanted to throw a puke bowl at her.

"I asked the doctor a half an hour ago for an update on my husband."

"Your husband is Lucian, right?"

She was smiling and on a first-name basis with him, so I knew he was fine. From the blush hitting her cheeks and the glimmer in her eye, I could tell he'd been laying the charm on from his damned hospital bed.

"Yes," I said pointedly.

"He's doing really well. They've done an MRI and it was clear, so they're running more blood tests now. We're just waiting for the results."

"Can I go see him? Can you wheel me to him?"

"Sure. He's a little loopy, just so you know. He's on a high dosage of anti-seizure and pain medication."

I just shrugged, so she left the room and returned a moment later with a wheelchair. She wheeled me to the last room at the end of the hall. There he was, looking so mortal with an IV, a hospital gown, and a loopy grin.

"Heya, gorgeous," he slurred.

I was wearing hospital-issued underwear, a giant Maxi pad, and a backless hospital gown, but I didn't care. I crawled into his bed, right into the crook of his arm where I've always existed.

"Ah, come here," he said, kissing my forehead and pulling me closer.

Pepto Nurse tried to object, but Lucian put his finger to his mouth and nodded. She left the room without a word. It was just the two of us.

"I'm so sorry, Evey." His voice was soothing.

"I know, me too. I don't think we can have a baby." I tried not to sob. "I don't even care anymore, and I don't want to go through that again. We need to find out what's happening to you. What if something is seriously wrong?" I whispered, "Your wings are gone."

"Things are changing. Something *is* wrong. And also you deserve a baby."

"Stop it. What are you not telling me? I'm torn up about

this, all of it, but mostly about what's happening to you. Tell me what's going on."

For a moment, I thought that Lucian was finally going explain to me the meaning of life or why he and I were in that situation. He was staring into my eyes with so much warmth and love in his expression, but then he just smiled and said, "Let's cuddle. These drugs are good."

"Lucian, tell me anything, something. I need to know." I started to sit up to examine him.

He pulled me back down and shook his head. Lifting the blanket back to reveal his feet, he gestured toward the end of the bed and said, "See?"

Lucian had had the sexiest man feet I'd ever seen, but they had become pale, almost bluish. "What's wrong?"

"I don't know."

A moment later, a doctor came in holding paperwork. It was the same guy who had been treating me. "Oh, hello. I see you found your husband."

"Yes, no thanks to you," I replied, looking away.

Lucian squeezed me tighter.

"Yes, I'm sorry about that," the doctor said. "We were going over the results of his blood work. There really is no concrete explanation for your seizure. Your levels look fine—"

"Show him your feet, Lucian."

The doctor quirked an eyebrow, but he checked Lucian's feet. "Hmm. I've never seen anything like this. Is it painful?"

"Not at the moment," Lucian responded.

"We'll keep you overnight for more observation, and I'll prescribe you a low-dose seizure medication until we can figure out what's going on."

We both nodded.

After the doctor left, Lucian and I began to doze off.

Just before I fell asleep, Lucian said, "Evelyn, we do have to figure things out."

"Tomorrow," I told him. Now we were both playing the denial game.

18

THREE STEPS BACK

Lucian

"IT'S TOMORROW, EVEY," I said, sitting next to the hospital bed she was sleeping in. "Wake up, talk to me."

She groaned and rolled over. "I don't want to talk."

I had gotten dressed and gathered our things. We were being discharged at the same time. Evey's mom came into the room before Evey and I could start the conversation I knew we needed to have.

I stood up. "Hello, Jane."

A second later, Jane was crying in my arms. "I'm so sorry for both of you. Why didn't you call me yesterday?"

The truth was that we weren't thinking about anything but ourselves. Evey and I hadn't thought to call her parents or Brooklyn. We'd just needed to be alone. We still needed time to figure everything out.

An image ran through my mind of Evey playing with her dolls in her bedroom in Oakland. She was about six, and she would feed and change and care for her dolls as though they were real babies.

Once when she was even younger, she asked Mrs. Obernickle, her preschool teacher, why she didn't have a family. Mrs. Obernickle responded with something harsh like, "Having children isn't like having dollies, Evelyn, don't be silly. They require much more work."

I'd thought it was such a harsh response, and Evey's face scrunched up with sadness. She became disappointed about life and her future in an instant. And because I had no self-control with Evey, I refused to let her childhood heart be broken by a cynical and grumpy old woman.

That day I had moved into Mrs. Obernickle's tubby body, with her stinky perfume, and knelt next to Evey and said, "But you will be a wonderful mother. Look at all the practice you're getting now with your dollies. You have nothing to worry about. Babies and children are a joy and a blessing."

She had smiled and hugged me—or hugged Mrs. Obernickle rather. Evey had always wanted to be a mother.

In that cold, sterile hospital room, I watched her trying her hardest to put on a brave face. But I could always see right through her, into her soul. I could see and feel the pain she was enduring after losing another baby. It was all my fault, and I might have been dying from the guilt alone.

"Mom," Evey said from her bed. Jane turned to face her daughter. "I'm sorry we didn't call you. They were running tests on Lucian, and I was feeling terrible."

"I know, DD, but I could have been here for you both."

They hugged. Evey hadn't been terribly close to her mother growing up. There was a lot of pressure on Evey to be perfect, especially from her mom, but I was sensing a change in both of them. Jane turned back to me. "Have they figured out why you had a seizure, you poor thing?"

"No. No explanation. Just a fluke, I guess." *Well, Jane, you see, I'm a guardian angel who is probably experiencing some sort of cosmic breakdown that is affecting the physical body I hang out in.*

"It's a very serious thing, you know?" She brushed my cheek with her smooth hand. In that moment, I wished I had had a mother.

"I know. I'm scared."

She hugged me for the second time that day. "Don't be scared. They'll figure it out. Have faith."

That word again.

Evey's father entered the room and went straight to Evey. They had always been a lot closer than Evey and her mother. "Ah, DD, I'm so sorry, sweetie."

Evey started crying. "I'm sorry too, Dad. I wanted to give you guys a grandchild so bad."

Each word in that sentence felt like a knife being thrust into the center of my chest. With me, Evey would never be able to give her parents a grandchild; I knew that, and I was finally able to admit it.

A WEEK WENT by, then two, then three. We were able to clean

up the loft and move in. It still needed a lot of work to make it the perfect work/living space, but Evey was knocking it out with relentless energy. I had never seen her so independent and determined. She was growing up... changing. Sometimes I felt like she didn't need me anymore, like I was just a boat anchor holding her back. In a matter of a few months, Evey had gone from relying on Tracey and Brooklyn for everything, to getting what she needed done, all on her own. She'd also never stood up for herself the way she did now.

We hadn't talked about anything serious since our last day in the hospital. We spent our time working on the loft and getting ready for Brooklyn's wedding. Every day, I got weaker and weaker, but I kept it to myself. I hadn't had another seizure. I also hadn't told Evey anything about what I had heard that day while I was seizing on the floor of the San Francisco General Hospital lobby.

The night before Brooklyn's wedding, I collapsed in the stairwell of the loft building. The elevator was being serviced, so I had to climb three flights. I was heaving and out of breath when Evey found me.

"What's going on, Lucian?"

Holding my chest, I said, "I just need to catch my breath. I'll be okay."

She helped me to the top of the stairs, where we both sat.

"I'm ready to talk," she said.

"Did you finish the speech for Brooke's wedding?"

"Not about that."

I shook my head and lifted my pant leg to reveal my calves, which had also begun to turn pale and bluish. "I have to tell you something."

She nodded, eyes wide.

"When I had the seizure, I heard a voice."

"Whose voice?"

"I'm not sure." That was the truth.

"What did the voice say?"

It was hard to explain. "It wasn't words. Just sounds, like frequencies and chanting."

"What does it mean?" she asked irritably.

"Those were the sounds I heard when I was made. When I was born."

"I don't understand."

Turning my body toward her, I touched my fingertips to her neck and felt her fast pulse. I tried to use my energy to calm her down. "Evey, they're calling me back."

"You're dying," she said immediately. It wasn't a question. She already knew.

"I think so."

"But you're responding to the medication. Maybe a doctor or a specialist can help you."

"No, Evey." I pulled her head into my chest. "Not this time, my girl."

She pulled away and scowled. "No, I won't let this happen. We have to try."

What I knew that I couldn't explain to her was that the sounds I'd heard calling me back were not asking for permission. I didn't have a choice. I was silenced by whatever had created me.

"Evelyn, listen to me, when I'm gone, you won't remember any of this. You'll go on."

"You've said that already. But I don't want to go on without you."

"You won't know anything else. You won't remember. Believe me."

"What if I do?"

"You won't." I couldn't bear to see her like this. I wanted to end it all right there, but I was a coward. "I should not have done this to you."

"What will happen to your soul when you're gone? Will I see you again?" she asked.

"I don't know if I have a soul, Evey."

Shaking her head, she stood and ran inside the loft. On the other side of the door, she yelled, "Yes, you do, you bastard."

She didn't speak to me for the rest of the day. Instead, she worked on her speech for Brooklyn's wedding.

At dinner, I asked, "Do you want to read it to me to practice?"

"No thanks. I need to get used to being alone."

"Evey…"

"You're giving up. Don't talk to me."

"I'm not doing anything," I argued.

"Exactly. I'm going out to pick up my dress at the seamstress's."

"I'm going with you."

She shot me a derisive look. "You're exhausted, Lucian. Just stay here. I don't want to be around you anyway."

"I have to. I still need to protect you."

"You couldn't protect a puppy at this point."

Ouch.

I tried to cloak myself, but I was no longer able to. Following her out onto the street, I stayed back and tried to pop into the body of a female mail carrier going in the same direction, but I failed at that as well. My concentration was shot, and I had no energy.

Halfway down the block, Evey turned around and yelled at me. "I said leave me alone."

I had to jog to catch up to her. I was out of breath. "Pl- please don't do this."

She stopped walking and turned to face me. Looking at me pointedly, she said, "Go home before I scream and have you arrested."

I shook my head in disbelief. I thought about all of the things I had done to her. I had confused her about life and God and the world. I caused her to suffer two miscarriages, and now she had to watch the person she loved get weaker and weaker every day. She was already grieving me, and I wasn't even gone yet.

I looked down the street and saw a bus approaching. Poof. That was all it would take, but like I said, I was a coward.

I went home feeling like I was dragging a dead body behind me. A series of images ran through my mind on a steady loop: Evey getting mugged, shot, hit by a car, assaulted.

In the bathroom, I tried to use a cold cloth to bring my fever down, but nothing worked. It was spiking and I was dizzy. I threw up and then collapsed near the tub.

Isn't love supposed to be easy? Isn't love supposed to be fun? The moment you fall in love, you become acutely aware of all the different ways the person you love can die. It's sickening. It's morbid and painful and heart-wrenching, and it's all totally, completely worth it.

My brave and cocky façade had been gone for months. I

was a weak body, withering away right in front of Evey's eyes.

I stayed on the floor, trembling until she returned. I heard the sounds again, calling me, and felt a pull like the type of pull I'd felt to be near Evey before I started getting sick.

When Evey got home, she came into the bathroom and immediately bent and felt my forehead. "You need to get into the tub. You need a cold bath."

My teeth chattered. "I'm freezing already."

"Lucian, just listen to me. Do as I say please, or I will call an ambulance."

While she ran the bath, I tried to smile at her, but she just looked away.

"You've been making a lot of threats today, young lady," I told her, trying to lighten the mood.

"If you think I'm going to let you dissipate into a plume of dust to be forgotten forever, you're crazy."

She undressed me and helped me into the tub. Poor Evey still had hope. She still had faith that we'd be together. It was too bad that I had none.

She sat on a stool next to the tub and washed my hair. I was shivering uncontrollably. When Evey said that my fever had passed, she ran warm water over my skin. I felt my body become balanced and strong enough to stand.

She helped me to our bed and brought me soup before lying down next to me. "You're a stubborn, recalcitrant man."

"That's a big word. You know I taught you that word?"

"No Charlie—oh yeah, it probably was you."

"I'm guessing you've been called that more than a few times." She laughed finally. She was trying to lighten the mood. I've heard angels singing for real. Her laughter sounded ten times better.

"Some guardian angel I am, huh?" I tried to feed her a spoonful of soup, but she waved it away.

"You could use some work on your angel skills. Will you please go to the doctor on Monday?"

"Okay," I said, but I knew it would be pointless. Just like anyone else, I had no control over when I'd be taken, and I knew there was no medical help for me.

I would just stick around and try to collect smiles from her. I'd put them all inside myself and try to build my own little pathetic soul from the love she had given me.

AT BROOKLYN'S WEDDING the next day, more than a few people asked if I was feeling okay. Evey looked stunning even though Brooklyn had chosen a hot pink mini-dress and cowboy boots for her bridesmaids. I kept to myself for most of the wedding while Evey did her matron of honor duties, though she checked on me every ten minutes.

When it was time for her to give the speech, I watched her take the microphone and scour the room for me. Her eyes locked on mine. "Thank you all for coming. I am so happy for Brooklyn and Keith and honored to be a part of this special day. I've known Brooklyn for most of my life. She's my best friend, but she is and always will be a real pain in my ass too."

The crowd gasped, but I started laughing.

Evey went on. "She means well, some of the time, but I

think instead of a toast, right now Brooklyn needs a roast, even if it is at her own wedding. So here it is, Brooklyn booger picker. That was her nickname in the third grade." Evey looked at her notes then looked up again. "Oh, and by the way, this was the third speech that I wrote for Brooke. The first went on and on about what a good friend she's been to me—not all true—and the second version talked about love and sacrifice and how thanks to Lucian"—she winked at me—"I finally know what that means. But I want to be real with you all. The truth is that Keith is an angel, a real angel for taking this girl on."

Evey jutted a thumb in Brooklyn's direction while she continued staring at me. She laughed then turned toward Keith, who was smiling kindly at her. The audience was chuckling, and of course Brooklyn looked furious.

"First of all, you're going to have to learn to do dishes, sweet Keith, because our darling Brooklyn will never, in her life, do a dish. She might cook for you—though she has a habit of eating the entire meal before it's finished—but dishes... forget it."

The crowd was in hysterics.

Evey looked back at Brooklyn, who was not happy. "I say most of this with a light heart because Brooklyn is the sister I never had. We can tell each other anything, and we've been there for one another for a long time and I know we always will be. This year we made a lot of changes." She finally addressed Brooklyn directly. "I'm proud of us, Brooke, for finally growing up, putting an end to our codependency issues, and finding two awesome guys to share our lives with. I love you so much, and I can't wait to see where life takes us."

Everyone clapped. Evey went over and hugged a smiling Brooklyn. We were going through so much unknown crap, but Evey was selflessly there for her friend through all of Brooke's bridezilla moments during the planning process. I hadn't expected the roast, but after hearing her words, I realized that both girls had come a long way. I was proud to see Evey standing up to Brooklyn and to see Brooklyn finally showing some much-deserved appreciation for her best friend.

As I sat there watching the girls dance, memories swirled around in my head. I thought back to a day in the park when Evey was playing chess with Charlie. She was maybe ten years old and her mom was sitting on a bench close by, watching her. Evey was an excellent chess player from a young age. She had gotten so good that she could beat her mom and dad, so her mom would take her to the park to play against Charlie. He was a good teacher for a while, but he could be grumpy. He was also experiencing the very early stages of dementia, so I'd pop into his body once in a while to give Evey more of a challenge.

"Ah, no, Evey. Think about that move. You need to be thinking about my next five moves," I had said.

"But I don't know what you're going to choose to do, Charlie."

"By moving your bishop across the board for a lousy pawn, you'll expose your queen. See here. It's not worth it. I'll have your queen in three moves."

"Hmmm." She scratched her little chin like she was years wiser than me.

"Evelyn, did you know that the knights aren't allowed to be next to the queen because she thinks the horses stink?"

"Everyone knows that."

Ha! My smart girl.

She was staring at the board, concentrating on her next move. "I can't decide if I should move my knight or one of these little dudes."

"They're called pawns, luv."

"I know, but I want to call them little dudes."

I smiled at her. "Call them whatever you want. You know what I think? I think if there was a princess in the game of chess, she'd look just like you."

She giggled. "Charlie, how come you don't have a wife or kids?"

"What was that?" I asked then popped out of Charlie's body. I didn't know the answer.

Evey repeated, "How come you don't have a wife and kids, Charlie?"

"I don't know, luv. I guess I wanted a career. I spent a lot of time working and just didn't see how a family would fit in."

I watched with trepidation, not knowing how the conversation would affect Evey.

"Why can't you have both?" Evey asked.

"Well, sometimes if you want to be really good at something or really successful, there isn't much time for the monotony of domestic life." He scratched his mustache and studied the chessboard.

He put his hand on the rook and Evey said, "But you'll expose your queen if you do that."

Charlie looked at her and laughed. "Well, aren't you the little grandmaster."

"It's what you just taught me."

He nodded, still watching the chessboard.

"Charlie, do you get lonely now that you're retired and don't have a family?"

He seemed to be getting agitated by her line of questioning. I wondered if I should intervene. "Sometimes, kid, family is just added weight keeping you down."

Evey scowled before glancing at her mother on the bench. She was offended and rightfully so. I'd had enough. I moved into Charlie's crummy old body. "I'm just kidding. You can have it all, especially because you're smart, my little princess."

That earned me an Evey smile. Or at least it earned Charlie one.

I knew then that Evey would be the love of my life, but I didn't know that I would be hers... that *I* would be her family. Back then, it wasn't a thought in my mind. I just wanted Evey to grow up and have everything she wanted. All I cared about was her happiness.

All I care about now is her happiness, yet here I am, keeping her to myself and hurting her with each day that passes in this unchartered world we've created.

AFTER BROOKE'S WEDDING, Evey lay naked in my arms, in our bed that faced the giant windows looking out to the city.

"I loved your speech. I didn't expect that."

"She had it coming," Evey said groggily. "You're tired, aren't you?"

"It's late."

"No, I mean, you're tired. You're weak."

I rolled over on top of her and used my index finger to trace a line down the side of her face and over her plump, pink lips. "Never too tired for this."

19

CONSEQUENCES

Evelyn

HE TOUCHED HIS lips to mine and kissed me softly as he caressed my neck and shoulder.

"Lucian... you don't have to."

"I want you, Evey. I'll always want you."

Time stopped. We were nothing but bodies loving and touching each other. We were two people, two humans in love, making love. He was young again, just a man, a beautiful, sensual, strong man.

He went up on his knees, leaving my body so he could sit back on his heels. I was waiting, open to him as he stared down at me.

"You are the sexiest thing. I can't get enough of you," he said, his voice thoughtful and soft.

A moment later he was inside of me again, thrusting harder, kissing rougher. "Ah, Lucian."

"I want to die doing this to you," he whispered near my ear.

"You might get your wish if you don't slow down." I felt a climbing ache; I could hear my hard breaths.

He slowed. "I want this to last forever."

"I can't hold on," I breathed.

He held my head, kissing and sucking at my lips and neck, while he moved in and out with perfect force and rhythm. He never let up.

Nothing would ever feel as good as being loved by him.

IN THE MORNING, I heard Lucian tinkering in the kitchen. I could smell coffee and toast. I smiled before opening my eyes and spotting him across the loft. As if he still had that special connection, he turned around and smiled back at me. He was shirtless in flannel pajama bottoms; his body was a work of art. Even though he was weaker than before, he was still so beautiful to look at.

"Come here," he said.

Wearing one of Lucian's white T-shirts, I skipped over to the kitchen area and hopped up on the counter. He stood between my legs and ran his hands up my thighs.

"Hello, handsome."

"Good morning, gorgeous," he said, before kissing me.

I pulled away. "How are you feeling?" I linked my

legs behind him.

"I'm okay. Better now that you're wrapped around me. Hungry?" He reached behind me, grabbed a plate of toast and avocado, and handed it to me.

"Thank you," I said.

There was some kind of resignation in his demeanor. I would have mistaken it for contentment had I not known how troubled he had been just days before.

"What are you thinking, Evey?"

"Wouldn't you like to know?"

"Always have. Always will," he said.

"I was thinking that you seem different this morning."

"How so?"

I frowned. "Defeated."

He shook his head. "Not defeated. I'm not surrendering in the way you think I am. There's no white flag here. I'm not going to apologize because I love someone. No one should be punished for giving love and getting it in return, even if others think it's wrong. How can two able-minded adults loving each other ever be wrong? It makes no sense."

I pecked his lips and smiled. "It's never felt wrong to me."

"I don't know what's happening, why I'm getting weaker and weaker. I don't think I'm becoming a normal man at all. And if this is God's way of punishing me because I love you, the person I was meant to love and protect, then I want nothing to do with him."

"Can't you talk to him?"

"I don't think it works that way. Anyway, I've been talking to him for years. So have you. Look where that's gotten us."

It pained me to hear Lucian being so cynical. I felt my

eyes welling up. "Please don't be so negative. Anything is possible. Don't lose faith."

"You are good through and through, Evelyn Marie Casey. Even now when you've been put through so much. I'm not surprised. You've always been good, always cared for people."

"You helped me become who I am."

"I don't know anymore if that's true," he said.

"You did." My heart was breaking, one small crack at a time.

He smiled finally. "Well, let's not dwell on it anymore. I'm tired of thinking about it all."

"Me too." I was relieved to see his mood change.

"Want to get out today and go do something? Maybe wine tasting?" He wiggled his eyebrows.

"Yes, please!" I opened my eyes wide.

"I'm gonna shower."

"I'll be there in a minute. I'm gonna eat my yummy toast," I sang to him.

He walked away toward the bathroom. I watched the flexing muscles of his back, where once there had been beautiful wings. It all seemed impossible now. He was my husband. I smiled at the memory of the night before... his hands, his lips all over me.

Everything changed a moment later when I heard a loud crashing sound come from the bathroom. I ran and pushed the door open to find Lucian lying unconscious on the floor.

"No!" I got onto my knees and shook him, but he was limp. "Lucian! Wake up."

He was wedged between the door and the tub, the water from the shower splashing onto his face. He seemed so fragile, like he could disappear right there in my arms.

I got up and ran for the phone. It felt like it took ten minutes for me to cross the loft and grab it, but it was probably two seconds. I dialed 9-1-1.

"9-1-1, what's your emergency?"

"My husband..." I couldn't catch my breath as I ran back to the bathroom. Kneeling next to Lucian's body, I scanned him for injuries and tried to continue. "He..."

"Take a breath, ma'am."

"I'm trying. My husband... collapsed in the bathroom. I don't know what's wrong. He's unconscious."

"Can you tell if he's breathing?"

"I don't know," I said. "I can't tell."

"Put your hand behind his neck and check his airway by putting your ear near his mouth and your hand on his chest."

"He's breathing, I think."

"Okay, just keep him still and keep his airway open." I gave them my address and apartment number, though I felt like I was slurring my speech. It was hard to catch my breath. "We have emergency responders on the way. Are there any pets in the home?"

"No," I breathed. *We could have gotten a puppy. We should have gotten a puppy.*

"Can you make sure that the emergency responders have access to your building?"

"Yes. We're on the third floor, unit two." I set the phone down and carefully removed my hand from behind Lucian's neck.

I ran and propped the door open, then I went to the stairwell and propped that door open as well. I jogged down the stairs as fast as I could into the lobby of the building, where a man was sitting on the bench.

"S'cuse me," I said, breathing hard. "Can you let the emergency responders in?"

He nodded. He said nothing to me, just a nod. *Is he my new angel? Is this the end for Lucian?*

I ran back up the stairs, back to Lucian. I took him in my arms and finally broke down and cried.

"Ev..."

I pulled away and looked at his face. "Lucian?"

He was groggy. "I'm still here." Then he lost consciousness again.

"No, wake up, please."

When the paramedics arrived, I was hysterical and hyperventilating.

One of them tried to calm me down. I screamed. "God, stop this!"

They plugged him into all of their machines and lifted him onto a gurney. They said his blood pressure was low. His condition seemed to be worsening rapidly. They put stickers on his chest and someone said, "Clear," and his body jerked. They were trying to save his life. I was in shock.

Words were being thrown around, none of which I understood. I followed the paramedics to the van and hopped in the back.

Holding Lucian's hand, I prayed while the two men worked on stabilizing him. They asked me about his medical history, but what could I say?

"I don't know. We've never talked about it. He had a seizure a few weeks ago. They did tests but didn't find anything. Please, please help him."

"We're doing everything we can, ma'am."

In the hospital, they did their best to stabilize him. I stayed beside him all day, and he finally regained consciousness at four in the afternoon.

"What's happening?" he said.

I was standing near the head of the bed. "They don't know. They're running tests. They've given you medicine to regulate your blood pressure."

Somehow he had enough strength to pull me down onto the bed with him. "I'm okay, Evey. I'm still here, aren't I?"

"Your heart was going crazy."

"You own my heart, lady." He smiled weakly.

"How much time do you think you have?"

As sick as Lucian was, he still got a laugh out of that. "Like anything else, who the knows? Who the hell knows? Will you promise me something, Evey?"

"Anything." I kissed his cheek and nuzzled into his neck.

"Promise me that if you remember anything after I'm gone, you'll protect yourself by not speaking a word of it. There's no telling what could happen."

"I would never."

"Also, you have to live a normal life for me. Please." He squinted, smiling with his eyes. "I worked so hard to make sure you had a normal life. I wish I could control myself with you. I wish I hadn't done this to you. I'm sorry."

"You said no apologies. You can't fault a person for love, and you're still here."

Just when I said that, he looked like he was going to pass out. An alarm went off on the screen above his bed. I ran to get the nurse.

20

LAST CALL

Lucian

I FELT WOOZY. An alarm was beeping above my bed. Evey had run out to get help. On the other side of the darkened room, I noticed a figure sitting in the chair.

"Mona?"

She stood and came to me. "Well, you got your wish."

"I didn't wish for this, to die this way."

"I mean you got yourself an appointment with Him." She pointed at the ceiling. "A face-to-face, a sit-down, Lucian."

That angered me. "Oh what, now? So I die, and then I get to go talk to Him? What's the point of that?"

"To plead your case."

"To plead my case? You're not any less cryptic than you were two thousand years ago, Mona."

She put her hand on my arm, and I felt a surge of energy. "They're coming," she whispered. "I have to go."

She kissed my cheek, and then she was gone. The alarm stopped.

"False alarm," I said when the doctor, nurse, and Evey all came rushing in.

"Oh thank God," Evey said.

"Don't thank him." I smirked.

The doctor and nurse checked me out thoroughly before leaving the room. The doctors were all stupefied by my case. I think the fact that they couldn't figure out what was wrong with a seemingly healthy thirty-year-old man, bruised their egos a little.

They stopped giving Evey updates. I think they were just trying to keep me alive.

I coded again later that day. The only thing I remember about it was that Evey was screaming. Later that night, I woke when I overheard a doctor telling Evey I was septic and that my body wanted to die.

Evey lay beside me and cried. I drifted in and out of consciousness. I tried to hold her and comfort her, but I couldn't anymore. I was only hurting her. At one point I asked her to call her mom, but she refused.

"No," she said. "It's too complicated, and I don't feel like lying to them anymore."

"I understand. I just don't want you to be alone. I love you so much. For two thousand years, I had no life. You gave me life, and I'm grateful to you." I kissed her and she kissed me back, and then she began sobbing again. "Please say something to me."

She sniffled and tried to calm down. "I don't know

whether I'm alive or dead, in heaven or hell or if any of this is even real. I just know that I love you, Lucian."

The alarms went off.

Poof.

21

CAREER, LOFT, RELATIONSHIP

Evelyn

"HEY, PINKY, WAKE up!"

I opened my eyes to find Brooklyn hovering over me. "What are you doing here, and how'd you get into my loft?"

She smiled. "I stole your key the other day and made a copy for myself." She tried to lean down and kiss me.

"Ew, get off me." I glanced at the clock. It was six thirty on a Saturday. "I'm going to kill you. Seriously, why are you here? I was up all night sketching. I wanted to sleep in."

"Well, first of all, don't you miss me?"

I rolled my eyes. "And second of all?"

"Second of all, you should be out on dates on a Friday night, not held up in your loft, drawing."

"This coming from a woman who wouldn't go out with the same person twice. Now you're married and the expert?" She was right though. I should have been out dating.

"You know I'm right." She looked around the room. "Your loft looks amazing. I can't believe you did all of this yourself."

"Well, I don't date, remember? I have plenty of time on my hands."

"We can fix that." She wiggled her eyebrows.

"Please don't set me up. You know I hate being set up." I got up to head to the kitchen to make coffee. Brooklyn followed close behind. "You want some coffee?"

"I already had my daily allowance."

Turning around in the kitchen area, I glared at her. "What are you talking about?"

She grinned from ear to ear and batted her eyelashes. I looked down at her stomach. "Are you serious? Are you pregnant?"

When she nodded, I grabbed her and squeezed her. I felt her start to cry.

"You're gonna be an auntie," she said.

"I can't wait." I was getting emotional too. As happy as I was, I felt an emptiness inside of me that I couldn't explain—a void. I was envious of Brooklyn for the first time in a long time.

She pulled out of the hug and wiped the tears from her cheeks. "It's still early, but I wanted to tell you first—after Keith, of course. I haven't even told my parents."

"Brooke, I'm honored. I want to be there for you every step of the way. I know I've been so busy lately and I haven't been the greatest friend. I was just swept up with the loft and my new line. I feel like I've been living in a social fog the last few months."

"It's okay, pinky. By the way, how is the line coming along?"

Brooke never used to care, so I stared at her before I answered. "You're never going to believe this. Divine Denim is being featured in next month's *Vogue*." I started jumping up and down. "It comes out in two weeks. Ah!"

Brooke started jumping too.

"Don't jump... the baby."

"Oh yeah." She laughed. "Ah, Evey, I'm so proud of you."

We hugged again. I didn't ask for my key back, and I promised myself I'd be more open to dating. My career was taking off, I had a place of my own... it was time.

0

BACK TO ZERO

Lucian

IS THAT BEEPING? What is that beeping? I felt a nudge, and then a full-out kick in the back of my leg.

"Ouch!"

"Lucian, your fucking phone is ringing. Answer it. It's probably your mother."

Groggily, I sat up and reached for my phone. "Hi, Mom."

"Hi!" Her voice was so cheery that it always put a smile on my face, even when my irritated girlfriend was glaring at me.

"What's up, Mom?"

"Is Laura there?"

"She is."

"Oh." Her voice fell.

I stood, walked into the kitchen, and pushed a stack of bills out of the way so I could start a pot of coffee. "What's going on? You can tell me."

"I was just gonna see if you wanted to get brunch."

"Brunch sounds great." Several seconds of silence passed. I lowered my voice. "I know you don't like her, Mom, she's probably going to work. It'll just be us."

"It's not that I don't like her. I'm a mom, your mom, and I think you deserve the best."

My mother and father had the ultimate relationship. They had been best friends for thirty-five years until he passed away last year of cancer. After his death, my mother became hyper-focused on my life.

"Mother, I'm jobless, living in a shitty one-bedroom apartment—"

"You're going to get a job. You have too much talent not to. Things will turn around for you." She whispered, "Laura doesn't treat you well, Lucian."

Laura was always harping on me about getting a regular job, but I had gone to college for graphic and web design. I wasn't giving up on that. It was a real job, and I'd had one until there were cutbacks where I had been working. It wasn't my fault at all. I had been unemployed for seven months, living in a fog. I was just going through the motions with Laura, who I had met and started dating in college. She had gone on to med school, and now she was a hotshot surgeon at San Francisco General. I only saw her two days a week, and we usually spent it fighting.

"I'll meet you for brunch. Where should we go?" I asked my mom.

"Meet me at Sweet Maple. I'm buying."

I sighed. "Okay. I'll meet you there in an hour."

Shuffling back into my room, I heard Laura on the phone, talking to someone about one of her patients. "I'll be in shortly," she said.

I was relieved that I wouldn't have to make up an excuse to leave.

Laura had long, straight blond hair, a narrow chin and nose, and big pink lips. She was six feet tall, only two inches shorter than me, and had a killer body. I used to think she was model-ish and unique; now she reminded me of a Viking warrior. There was no softness to her, mentally or physically.

Inside the room, I slid back into bed while she scrolled through her phone. Without looking over, she said, "I have to go in today. One of my patients is having some post-op issues. You going to brunch with your mom?"

"How'd you know?"

"Because you do that on Saturdays."

"You work a lot on Saturdays."

She ignored that. "They're hiring orderlies at the hospital."

I laughed through my nose, and then turned on my side to face her. She was still looking at her phone. "I have a master's in design, Laura. I was making close to what you are when I got laid off."

"Then get a job."

I shook my head. "As though I haven't been trying."

"Try harder. My back is starting to hurt."

"What's that supposed to mean?"

"From carrying you. I pay for almost all of our meals out," she said.

"I always tell you I can't afford to go to the restaurants

you like anymore. I offer to cook for you. You insist on paying and act like it's no big deal."

She got up and tossed the covers back at me. "It's not a big deal when it comes to the money. It's the fact that doing it doesn't bother you."

"Are you serious? Are we living in the eighteen hundreds?"

She was standing naked and confident in front of my dresser mirror, brushing her long hair. "I have to go."

She went into the bathroom and started the shower. I followed her in and hopped up on the counter to talk to her through the shower curtain.

"We've been together for a long time, Laura."

"I know, and I love you. But things aren't moving forward for us anymore."

I agreed with her but stayed quiet.

"And..." she said.

"And what?"

"I had a spark with someone at my work."

"What in the world is a spark, Laura?"

"A connection. You know what a spark is."

I really didn't. "Are you cheating on me?"

She tore the shower curtain open and scowled. "Of course not. I've always been honest with you."

"Who is it?" I said.

"Another surgeon."

"Of course. Which one?" I knew a lot of the people she worked with.

"Tom." She blinked, expressionless.

"Really? Tom? He's like four inches shorter than you and how many years older... and he has no hair."

She shrugged. "We have a lot in common. Don't be so shallow."

"Outside of the fact that you make good money and enjoy cutting people open, what else do you have in common with him?"

Wrapped in a towel, Laura, who I had been with for seven years, broke up with me by simply saying, "We haven't really been a couple for a long time, Lucian. This will be like cutting out that fattening donut you have once a month."

She compared our relationship to a fucking donut. Or maybe she was comparing me to a fucking donut.

"A donut?"

She nodded. "A donut." She pecked me on the lips. "Good-bye. I hope we can always be friends."

Not likely.

After she left, I found myself standing there, still in the same spot in the bathroom, staring at the towel she had used. She said we hadn't been a couple in a long time. I thought about that remark the whole way to Sweet Maple.

When I got inside, my mother was already sitting at a table near the back. She stood to kiss me. Isla Bertrand was still a striking beauty at sixty-five, but it was her warmth that I always looked for in the women I wanted to date. I wasn't a mama's boy, but I didn't take her for granted either. She was my biggest fan, always there for me.

"Laura broke up with me," I said as my mother and I sat down. "She said we hadn't been a couple for a long time, and then she compared me to a donut." I opened my eyes wide and laughed. "Can you believe that? It's over. I'm a donut."

"Well, at least you're laughing about it." She took a deep breath.

My face fell. "You're relieved, aren't you?"

"I don't want to say I'm relieved. I just never felt like you and Laura were right for each other. Something was always missing."

"You mean like a spark?"

"Yes and love, real love. I think what you and Laura had was just for comfort, so you both could focus on your careers and not be distracted."

I tried to think back to when Laura and I had first met, how we'd felt about each other back then, but nothing stuck out in my memory. "You think we kept it together because it was comfortable?"

"Comfortable and easy." Her brow furrowed as she took my hand. "I'm sorry, Lucian. I know you've been together for a long time. Breaking up is never easy, even if you know it's for the best. Maybe you should take a year and just be single."

I scanned the menu and shrugged. "Maybe, although I've felt single for a long time."

"Love doesn't always have perfect timing. Just wait until you find the right person. Until then, live your life."

We ordered from the server, sipped coffee, reminisced about my dad, and then she couldn't help herself. "So any interviews coming up?"

"I don't want to jinx it," I said through a mouthful of French toast.

"Come on, you can tell your mom. Anyway, since when have you been superstitious? I could barely get you to go to church as a kid. I had to bribe you every Sunday."

"I'm not superstitious. I just don't want to get my hopes up. I have an interview next week with one of the top design agencies in the city. They specialize in branding and shaping passion-based companies. They also work with some of the biggest green companies in the Bay Area. It'd be a dream job."

Her face practically exploded from happiness. "Oh, Lucian, that's wonderful."

"Mom, I haven't even gone to the interview yet."

"I know you'll get it."

"I should not have told you."

She smiled knowingly. "You've always been too hard on yourself. When you go to that interview, Lucian, be confident, be enthusiastic. That little bit of cockiness you had before wouldn't hurt either. Since you got laid off, that's all changed. You act undeserving. You can't help that the company was going under."

After brunch and a long talk, I kissed my mother goodbye and headed back toward my apartment. I was walking up the hill in the Mission toward my apartment, feeling guilty about not feeling guiltier about my relationship with Laura being over. Kenny, a guy I used to work with, called me and asked if I wanted to go out.

"Go out?"

"Yeah, rumor travels fast."

"What do you mean?"

"Laura told Cynthia what happened. Don't ever tell Laura this, but Cynthia was so happy. She was like, 'Good, now Lucian can find someone who doesn't treat him like shit.' Laura's just not nice, man."

"I know. I don't want to go out. I'm gonna go home and work on some new presentations. Dude, I have to get this job I'm interviewing for next week, or I'm going to run off to a monastery. No girl plus no job equals turn to God, right?"

We both laughed at that.

I STAYED INSIDE my apartment for a week working on my presentation. The morning of the interview, Laura came over to get some of her things. She acted nonchalant while she dug through my drawers, looking for random pairs of her underwear.

"Honestly, Laura, I'll mail them to you if I find any. I have to get going."

"Wow, Lucian, could you be any colder?"

"I have an interview."

Her eyes perked up. "Where?"

"None of your business. I mean, Laura, you're a gluten-free vegan." I pointed at my chest. "You don't need this fried dough. Be on your way now."

She was squinting at me and shaking her head. "What's gotten into you?"

"We're not going to be friends. So you can leave now."

"Your mom came into the hospital two days ago."

That stopped me in my tracks. "What? Why didn't I know about this?"

"She didn't want to stress you out."

Laura was such a conniving bitch. She wanted to sabotage everything for me. "Then why are you telling me now?"

"I just thought you should know. She wasn't feeling well.

She found a lump in her breast, and they're running a bunch of tests."

There was something strangely familiar about that news. Maybe like the day I discovered that my father had prostate cancer. I hated Laura for telling me that way, without a modicum of compassion. "Nice bedside manner. Get out of my apartment now."

"Seriously?"

"Yes, go now. You're heartless... empty... cold. I'm done talking to you."

"Now we're resorting to blatant insults? That's very mature."

"Really, just get out, please."

She left, huffing and puffing.

I checked the clock; I had to leave in ten minutes to make it to my interview on time. As if I could only move in slow motion, I dialed my mother's number.

"Big day for you," she said, sounding as chipper as ever.

"What's going on with your health? Laura told me—"

"Lucian, this is not your problem."

"You're my mother. It is my problem. Just tell me." I could feel myself breaking down. "Do you have cancer? I can't take two parents going through that within two years."

Her voice dropped, and she got serious as though she was scolding a little boy. "Listen to me. You go to that interview, and you hit it out of the park. And if you don't give it your all, what will that mean to me? I'll know in a few days what's going on in my body, and you will be the first person I tell. I promise. Until then, go get that job. For me, for yourself."

I couldn't say anything.

"Did you hear me, young man? Do not do this to me or to your father's wonderful legacy. He did not raise you this way. Keep it together."

I was on the verge of tears. I couldn't stop thinking about losing her. When I hung up, I looked at the clock. If I didn't literally run all the way to the building, I would be late.

Sprinting with my messenger bag under my arm, I made it into the lobby five minutes before my interview. It felt like the elevator was the slowest one I had ever been in. I tried to collect myself.

Once I hit the eighth floor, I made my way to the offices. The secretary flirted with me—I thought that couldn't hurt. I went into a large boardroom and did my presentation. It went by in a blur, but everyone clapped at the end.

Bradley, the man in charge, walked me out, slapping me hard on the back. "You did great, man."

"Thanks."

"You were our last interview. We've had a lot of really qualified applicants, but I could tell everyone in there liked you and the presentation."

As we headed toward the elevator, I tried to read between the lines and decipher what he was saying. Was he letting me off easy or was he telling me I got the job?

"We should have a decision by tomorrow," he said.

BLOWING OFF THE rest of the day drinking wasn't usually my style, but I had nothing else to do. I was a worried sick about my mom, who was spending the evening with her best friend.

Walking up the hill, I passed the Star Wars bar. I hadn't been in there in a while. I didn't recognize any of the bartenders. I sat on the tattered red vinyl stool.

"Two fingers? Scotch right?" the bartender asked.

"No, I'll just have a beer. I'll take that Belgian on tap."

The bartender shook his head. "I thought you were a whiskey guy. I must have mistaken you for someone else."

I had never seen the guy in my life, but I did think it was funny that he was dressed as Princess Leia. They usually didn't cross-dress at the Star Wars bar.

"What's your name?" he said.

"Lucian."

"I'm Zack." He shook my hand.

"Nice to meet you, man."

"So what brings you in?"

"I live close by," I said. "Just wanted to pop in for a beer."

"Ah, I see. Well, welcome."

I sat in that bar, thinking about what tomorrow would bring. Princess Leia wouldn't take his eyes off me. He kept shaking his head and making me feel really uncomfortable, so I decided to call it quits after two beers and head home.

I WOKE UP to my phone ringing at eight sharp. It was my mom.

"I'm clear. No cancer. Nothing. Just some benign, old lady crap."

I rubbed my face. "You're not old, Mom, but geez, I'm so relieved."

"Do you want to do brunch? You can tell me about the interview."

"I don't think I'm going to get the job. Just fair warning," I said, before rolling out of bed and heading to the kitchen to make coffee. Spotting a framed picture of Laura and me in Rome, I rolled my eyes. What a waste of seven years.

"Why don't you think you'll get the job?" she asked.

"Just haven't felt lucky lately."

"Don't be ridiculous. It's not about luck."

"I'm grateful for the good news I've already gotten today. Nothing could ruin that. Believe me, even if I don't get this job, I'll consider this a good day."

"Okay, honey, well, you'll keep trying if you don't. Let's go have a good meal. I feel revived."

I was smiling when I left my apartment to meet my mother. My phone started buzzing from my pocket. It was Bradley from the design firm. My heart sank a little, but I pulled it together, popped into an alley, cleared my throat, and answered.

"Hello, Lucian Bertrand."

"We all want you on our team. It was unanimous."

"You're kidding?" I tried to keep my voice steady as I acted like a teenage girl, jumping up and down in the alley.

"No, we're not kidding at all. We'd like you to start Monday. How do you feel about that?"

"I'll be there."

"Great, we'll see you then."

I almost hung up but caught myself and said, "Bradley, thank you so much! I'm truly psyched about this job."

"We know. Your talent was enough, but it was your enthusiasm that sold us all. Congratulations."

"Thank you."

I went skipping into the restaurant, and my mother knew. She jumped out of her seat. "You got it, didn't you?"

"I did."

"I told you." She cupped my face. "Good things always happen in threes."

We were laughing as we took our seats. "You said it's not about luck. Was number one Laura breaking it off with me?"

She smiled. "No, number one was that I am cancer-free. Number two was that you landed the job."

"And number three?"

"You'll have to wait and see." She winked. "Keep your heart open."

After brunch, I walked my mom home and then headed back up to the Mission. On my way, I passed a magazine rack. Browsing the design magazines, I felt an excitable presence next to me.

"Oh my God, is it here?" she asked.

Glancing over, my eyes met hers. She smiled, warmth radiating from her chocolate eyes.

"Hi," I said, a bit awestruck by her unique beauty.

"Hi. Sorry, do you mind? Can I squeeze in here and grab that?" It was a copy of *Vogue*.

"Of course," I said. "Although I can't actually say I've ever seen a person this excited over the latest copy of *Vogue*."

She laughed, and it sounded like music. "That's because my denim line is featured in it. Here it is! Ah!" She pointed at a page where some model was wearing Divine jeans.

"That's your line?" I looked up from the magazine

quickly, realizing I couldn't take my eyes off of her for more than a second. I didn't want her to leave. I was having eight thousand feelings all at once.

"Yes!" she said with so much excitement, it was contagious.

"That's amazing." I stuck out my hand. "I'm Lucian."

"Interesting name," she said.

"My mom got it from a romance novel."

She laughed. "I'm Evey."

When we shook hands, we shocked each other. We both pulled back. It was a spark.

Keep your heart open, Lucian. "We're electric together," I said.

"You're very confident. Not unlike those typical romance heroes."

"You're very perceptive."

"I've been told."

"So I'm not usually one to brag, but I sort of landed my dream job today, and you... you're in *Vogue* magazine. I think a celebration is in order. Want to grab a drink?"

"Yes! A hundred percent," she said.

She literally jumped into my arms and hugged me, and it didn't feel weird at all.

JUST THE
BEGINNING

Evelyn

YOU KNOW WHEN you meet someone, and you feel like you've know them your whole life, even though you know you've never once laid eyes on each other? That was how I felt with Lucian. No one could forget a face like his. He was gorgeous, exotic, with this French creamy skin and longish black hair and blue eyes. His smile was warm, and his personality made him instantly approachable.

We went out to dinner and celebrated on the first night we met. Halfway through the night, I had forgotten whether we were celebrating our career accomplishments or celebrating the fact that we had met each other.

"Tell me everything about you," he'd said.

He couldn't believe I had never had a serious boyfriend.

"I've just never met the right person."

"I get that. I was with someone for seven years, and really, it never felt like it would be forever." He paused, looking thoughtful. "I want to see you again, Evey."

"Really?"

"You just have this thing. You're beautiful and funny and smart, and I knew in five minutes I'd want to see you again."

"Do you believe in fate?" I asked him.

"I want to. I'm going to start right now. Can I eat dinner with you tomorrow?"

So soon, I thought? But that was old Evey talking. "Yes."

"And Monday?"

"Yes."

"Tuesday?"

I laughed. "Um, that might be pushing it."

"Yeah, you're right. I've had a lot of wine."

After the restaurant closed, Lucian walked me to the door of my building. "I get it though," I said.

"Get what?" He backed me against the glass lobby door and braced his hand on the back of my neck.

"How it feels to be with someone you really want to be around."

"Exactly," he said before pecking my lips. "See you tomorrow?"

I pulled him in and kissed him harder. "See you."

EPILOGUE

Mona

"LUCKY BASTARD," I said, as I twirled on the red barstool. The place was empty. It was magic hour and poor Zack couldn't leave, so I thought I'd pay him a visit. He was dressed as Chewbacca, except that he had removed the headpiece. He basically looked like an average guy wearing a fur onesie.

"He deserves it, Mona," Zack stressed. "Do you think I'll ever get out of here?"

"Zack, we let a lot slip with you."

"Can you get me a meeting? Like you got Lucian?"

"I don't know. I'll work on it."

"You know he came in the other day, ordered a beer?"

"Really? How'd he seem?" I asked.

"Good. He had no clue at all. Like, do they just zap him and then give him a backstory and all that crap?"

"No. He's always existed that way. That Lucian has

always been that Lucian."

"But he's the same."

"He is the same. Same soul. I don't know if time goes back, or if they're all created in our images, or we're created in theirs. One thing I do know now is that whatever faith you believe in, true love is real... and it endures. Look at Lucian and Evelyn and all that they went through. He must have pleaded a pretty good case."

Zack smirked. "I knew if anyone could pull it off, it'd be Lucian. I would have loved to have been a fly on the wall when he was talking to the big guy."

"Me too, Zack. Me too."

AUTHOR'S NOTE

Dear readers,

Thank you so much for reading *Lucian Divine*. I hope you enjoyed reading it as much as I enjoyed writing it.

If you'd like to help other readers find *Lucian Divine*, you can share the love and leave a review on Amazon, Goodreads, iTunes, Kobo, or Barnes & Noble. It is much appreciated!

If you're interested in reading my other novels, here's where you can find them and learn more... www.reneecarlino.com

Want news about my new releases before anyone else? Join my Facebook private group for giveaways and other exclusives... www.facebook.com/groups/381874001954996/

And finally, here are some other sites where we can TALK BOOKS!

Facebook:
www.facebook.com/AuthorReneeCarlino

Amazon Author Portal:
www.amazon.com/Renee-Carlino/e/B00CDXPNVI

Instagram:
https://instagram.com/reneecarlino1/

Twitter: @renayz

Peace, love, books, and chocolate!
Renée

ALSO BY
RENÉE CARLINO

Swear on This Life

Before We Were Strangers

Sweet Thing

Sweet Little Thing

Nowhere but Here

After the Rain

ACKNOWLEDGMENTS

Thank you, most importantly to the readers, the dreamers, the bloggers, the sharers, and all the other people who took a chance on this book. This was an adventure for me, something totally different. Your unwavering support is hugely appreciated.

There are people in my life who have continued to support and encourage me. It keeps me going every day. Thank you, Mom, Dad, Rich, Rachel, Donna and the gang. Friends and certain members of our extended family who share my book news, my Ya Yas, and the girls in my neighborhood, I am so grateful to you.

Rich and Donna, I should mention, in case you didn't read it, the kids probably shouldn't take this one to their school for show and tell.

And just because I get to say this, Little Johnny, you bring me joy.

Colleen, thank you for serenading me and for all the other awesome things you do. (Making fun of my Austin photo not included.)

Thank you also to Christina, The Jane Rotrosen agency, and Jhanteigh, who have been constant believers in this magical world of books, and also in me as a writer.

Whitney, thank you for all you do and for being so good to me.

Dallon, thank you for being there, and for that one line.

To the always enthusiastic Angie and Heather. You girls make me feel like the real deal. Angie, you kind of started this whole thing, and Heather, if I didn't think you had already found your calling, I would name at least three other jobs that you'd be the boss at. But what you're doing is the most important.

Kendall Ryan, I adore you. Thank you for helping me.

Rebecca, you we'rent the worst assistant. Though I will add that Allison was much better. Thank you both.

Caroline, thank you for laughing with me and sometimes crying with me and also for coining Cathlotica.

Dani, you kick ass! Plain and simple.

Cassie Cox, thank you for your editorial help.

Thank you to Brianna Harden for your cover design and talent!

Thank you Hang Le for your patience with me, and for your amazing work on the graphics.

Thank you to Angela from Fictional Formats for formatting for me at the drop of a hat.

Thank you to Christine Estevez and Karen Lawson for your proofing gifts.

Sam and Tony, thank you for helping me believe in the things I cannot see.

Finally to Anthony, my perfectly imperfect angel, heaven is here with you.

Made in the USA
Charleston, SC
22 January 2017